Silent Secrets

by

Mia O'Connell

Silent Secrets

Cover Art by *Jennifer Greeff*

The Wild Rose Press, Inc.
PO Box 708
Adams Basin, NY 14410-0708
Visit us at www.thewildrosepress.com

Publishing History
First Edition, 2022
Trade Paperback ISBN 978-1-5092-4379-2
Digital ISBN 978-1-5092-4380-8

Published in the United States of America

Dedication

To my daughter Megan, with love—you mean the world to me.

Prologue

July 2nd, 1998, Boston, Mass.
Rebecca

She was seven, proud, and wicked excited about this week. She didn't know what she was most pumped about, her parents taking her and her brothers to the fireworks at Boston Harbor, or getting to tag along with her big brothers to the playground at St. Anthony's across the street for the first time. Finally, she was considered a big kid. Rory, her oldest brother who'd just turned 13, didn't want anything to do with her; it just wasn't cool for a teen to be seen taking care of his little sister. Sean, only 10, knew how that felt so he took her hand and helped her across the street.

But as soon as the playground was in sight, Sean bolted when he saw his best friend, Andy. Rory bee-lined to meet up with his friends. One of them pulled out a pack of cigarettes. Rory pulled a lighter out of his back pocket. Big dummy-head, Rebecca thought, if Mom and Dad find out he's going to be so grounded.

Rebecca stopped to look up at the blue sky with big, fluffy clouds that looked like cotton candy. She imagined herself falling back and the clouds catching her. Rebecca spied a lone wild daisy, shooting up between the concrete slabs. She picked it and held it to her nose, too busy enjoying her favorite flower to notice the old station wagon with wood on the side pull up behind her.

"Hey, come to the window," a man's voice called out.

She turned and saw a bearded man with dark curly hair wearing dark glasses who sort of looked like her Uncle Tommy. His voice didn't sound like Uncle Tommy, and this wasn't Uncle Tommy's car, but then the man flashed a wide, happy grin.

"C'mere," he said, motioning with his head.

She approached the window, noticing it said Turbo on the side. Turbo, she thought, what a funny word. It sounded like a superhero! Sean would like the sound of that. She giggled, then peered inside and saw the man had no clothes on and his pee pee was standing straight up. She knew what a pee pee was—Rory and Sean called them wieners. She knew all about private parts, and she knew this man that looked like Uncle Tommy should be wearing pants.

She couldn't stop staring at his pee pee, confused at how it stood straight up. When she looked up at the man, he was smiling at her and licked his lips. The way he stared at her made her feel strange inside. Her legs felt strange, all wiggly and weak, and her mouth was closed tight as if it were locked. She watched as his hand moved up and down on his pee pee, and her face felt hot, like it was on fire. Her heart was pounding.

"Get in quick, or you'll be sorry. I'll hurt the other kids." His hand kept moving up and down. When she looked at him, his face turned mean, and she felt her hands shaking. Her mouth felt dry as sand, and her lips started to tremble as she tried to form words. She wanted to scream for Rory and Sean, but the sound was

In a lot of ways she was like the house—at one point she needed to be put back together and like her house, knew it was a process. She felt at home. She knew there was a story somewhere about this house, and she wanted to find out what it was. At night, she swore she heard a woman crying, and oddly, a child giggling. And this morning she'd swear something stroked her hair and woke her from a sound sleep. Maybe it was just her imagination getting the better of her but then again maybe not.

trapped in her head. She wanted to run, but her legs made no movement.

He leaned over, pulled the handle on the door, pushed it to open. In her head, she screamed for her legs to run, but her body wouldn't budge. She felt like a stick figure drawing stuck to a page. Out of the corner of her eye, she saw Sean, tried with all her might to will his name out of her mouth. She didn't want to get in, but she didn't want the other kids hurt. Her voice came out with a strangled "Seannnnn" sound. The man yanked her arm violently until she was half in and half out of the car. It hurt, she wanted him to stop, so she bit down hard on his arm and then felt him release. But then everything went dark.

Chapter 1

Burlington, Vermont
August 2016

God, she hated the process of moving. All her furniture sitting, waiting to be loaded, she was thankful she hired a local moving company to do the heavy lifting. Rebecca examined the last three boxes she would take with her, checked and rechecked their contents, and made a mental map of the trip north. She barely had the last box taped up when she heard the "Standells' Dirty Water" ringtone, a family favorite, blasting from her cellphone. The ringtone Rebecca had chosen for her brothers, Sean and Rory, before leaving Boston. Snatching her cellphone from her purse, she slid a finger across the screen which immediately filled with her two brothers' faces.

"ReRe, how's it going? Are you sure we can't come and help you with the big move?" Sean said, sitting in his man-cave wearing his favorite worn Boston Celtics T-shirt with cargo shorts and flip-flops. Rory, sporting a scruffy two-day-old beard, sat alongside him, blurry-eyed and from the look of it needing a strong hit of caffeine.

Rebecca couldn't help but grin at Sean's use of her childhood nickname, one he'd chosen for her when she was just a baby. She laughed as Sean elbowed his older brother, who in turn jumped awake and yawned.

"Yeah, Sean's right, we got nothing better to do. Fucking hot in Bean Town. Plus, Sean finally grew some muscles," Rory said, nailing Sean's arm with a punch.

Rebecca knew her brothers, and Rory's dig was payback for getting elbowed. "Guys, we've been over this. I'm all set. Take a look," she said, scanning the room with her phone. "Boxes are all packed and ready to be loaded."

"Re, you're not the only one with superpowers. Check out these guns."

Rebecca rolled her eyes at Sean, who flexed his muscles on screen.

"Seriously, dude, how old are you?" Rory joked, this time landing a punch on Sean's thigh.

"We can be there in no time," Sean said, ignoring his brother's taunt.

"Damn fucking straight. We can be there in two hours unless, of course, Sean drives, then it's more like five."

"Hey!" Sean protested, shouldering his brother.

"Yeah, and I'm reading you two assholes right now. You're both hiding from your wives to avoid doing chores." Rebecca saw the caught in the cookie jar look pass between them. "And besides, Rory, you look like hell. I wonder if sweet baby Conor is keeping you up at night? What am I thinking? Like that sweet little bundle of joy would keep anyone up."

"Bundle of joy? Not at two in the fucking morning—more like a bundle of screeching hell. And you know very well the Con-man is keeping me up! Don't be using that telepathic shit on me," Rory said with a hint of sarcasm.

"Too late, Rory. Seriously though, I love you both. I appreciate the offer."

Rebecca knew Rory's joke was a bit of a warning—you better stay out of my head or else! Like she had a choice in the matter. She knew her abilities freaked her older brothers out. It was hard for all of them to comprehend the unexplainable. One thing they all agreed on—she was never the same after the accident.

"If you change your mind, Re, you know where to find us. Love you," Sean said, blowing her a kiss before handing the phone to his brother.

"You better call us when you get settled, please," Rory said, his voice cracking slightly with emotion.

"I will, Rory, I promise. Please stop worrying about me."

Before putting her phone back in her purse, she glanced at her screensaver, a picture of her and her brothers at the Cape. Rory on her left, and Sean on her right, their arms wrapped protectively around her, holding on tight. Ever since the accident, she felt the weight of their guilt, physically and emotionally, in her body. Guilt for not paying attention and letting their little sister wander off, all those years ago at St. Anthony's. Both still trying to make up for what they could not change. Part of her decision to leave Boston for Burlington at eighteen was to push Rory and Sean to move on. Providing all of them with the necessary distance and space to breathe and, maybe, even to live a little.

And now, with the thought of her new life, the old baby blue cape, the acreage, and the peace and quiet of

Eden. She felt grounded. She packed up the remaining dog treats in a tote for the car, wrestled Lulu, her very opinionated tabby, into the cat carrier, took one last look around her old apartment, and locked the door. After she packed her car with the last of her things, loaded Lulu in, and settled her pups in the backseat, she programmed her navigation system for the trip north. A familiar tightness in her body and a growing pressure behind her eyes had her reaching for ibuprofen. Breathe, breathe, breathe through the tightness, through the discomfort, said the voice of her old therapist, Jayne Clemmons, in her head. She murmured to herself, "Slow it down, three deep breaths, and count to ten."

As she drove along Route 104, windows down, her dogs' heads out the car windows, Rebecca followed suit, breathing in all the smells of summer, and relished how the empty two-lane road before her lent itself to thinking. When her dogs Max and Manny began to whine, she pulled into the village store, a converted two-story house in Cambridge, Vermont, a good place to stretch her legs and let her pups out to pee.

Chapter 2

As she pulled into a parking spot and released her dogs from the backseat, Rebecca noticed him, the little boy, no more than six or seven, wearing a Red Sox T-shirt a couple of sizes too big. He sat alone on the store's steps, head down, throwing stones on the pavement below. The feeling of sorrow hit her like a truck, and Rebecca knew this little boy's soul was grieving. She walked over with her pups in tow. Manny stopped to nudge the little boy's foot with his nose. The little boy raised his head and peered his deep brown eyes into Manny's. Both held eye contact, passing between them the secret communication that occurs between dogs and children. Manny reached forward to give the little boy's nose one big sloppy kiss, and the little boy let out a big belly laugh, using the back of his hand to wipe at his mouth and nose.

"Can I pet him?" The little boy's eyes met Rebecca's and a flash of an image of him standing next to his mother's bed holding her hand bolted through her, causing Rebecca to exhale as if she had been holding her breath. She recovered by pressing her fingers to the bridge of her nose and said, "Sure, Manny loves a good rub, but you'd better pet Max too, or he'll get jealous." As the little boy sat flanked by two big German Shepherds, his small hands on each of their backs, she felt his grief ease up. He glimpsed briefly at her with a hint of a smile.

"I want a dog, but Dad said not now. He said I had to wait until Mama's done with her medicine. Her medicine made her hair fall out. I kinda laughed because she looks like a boy now. That's a secret, okay?" The little boy looked at Rebecca sheepishly.

"Okay, I can keep secrets. So can my pups. I'm Rebecca, and you've already made friends with Max and Manny."

"I'm Liam."

"Nice to meet you, Liam." As Rebecca sat down next to him, a man in his early thirties, running on fumes, rushed down the steps, carrying a box of saltine crackers in hand.

"Hey Liam, let's roll." The man's frantic energy headed toward her was palpable and intense. Rebecca sensed the overwhelming fatigue and the out-of-your-mind madness of dealing with a very sick wife and a small child alone.

"Dad, this is Rebecca and her dogs Max and Manny." The man stopped dead in his tracks, not even registering that his son was not alone. Bewildered he looked down at the two big dogs and then to Rebecca.

"Hey, hi, sorry, in a bit of a rush. We need to get back before his baby sister wakes up from her nap. Come on, little man, we gotta get home and give Mom her crackers."

"Bye, Rebecca. Bye, Manny. Bye, Max." Liam gave the dogs one last pat, held eye contact with Max for just a minute, and, with a fading grin, turned to leave.

"Bye, Liam, see you around," Rebecca said, giving Liam's hair a soft tousle. He turned and waved before running to catch up with his dad who was already behind the wheel. As the minivan pulled away, Rebecca sat for a moment in Liam's spot and gave a little prayer up to the universe for him and his family. Standing and stretching, she whistled to Max and Manny who were sprawled under a large maple tree and headed to the car.

As she merged back onto Route 104 heading east, thoughts of little Liam crowded her thinking. Her mind returned to the day when she was about Liam's age, seven to be exact, having survived a fall from the car. The aftermath, waking up after having spent seven weeks in a drug-induced coma to heal her body and her brain. Like Liam, she knew trauma changed a person, and her accident changed her. No longer a carefree seven-year-old, she'd woken up traumatized and scared.

From that day forward, she could feel and read other people's thoughts and emotions. She experienced it as psychic waves that gravitated towards her, with each individual wave holding information and images for her to decipher. She hid the secret from her family until she couldn't anymore. When Rebecca confided in her parents, they'd exchanged worried glances with the doctors. She remembered her mother's smile that day. The exact one her mother used when she was talking to someone she didn't care for. It reinforced Rebecca's belief that she'd been wrong in sharing her secret with them.

Rebecca spent a large portion of her childhood being evaluated at the Harvard Institute for Neuroscience after her accident. Her doctors recommended her for a research study, convincing her parents the study might shed light on her condition.

She'd hated the constant testing, the hours in the MRI machine, being forced to stay still. When she turned thirteen, she refused to go, tired of her life being orchestrated by a team of neurologists.

She wanted a life outside the hospital and daydreamed about being a typical teen. Doing normal teen things like her brothers did before her. The only problem was she had no friends. Her parents thought it best to homeschool her, their way to protect her from the outside world. Books became her best friends. Reading was one of the rare times her mind went still. She learned, early on, that getting lost in a good book was the best medicine to quiet her brain.

As she drove, she worked on shifting her focus from her past and her encounter with Liam and his dad to her current work projects as a publishing consultant. Her desire to grow her business would require her to branch out, maybe, even, re-brand her business model. She made a mental list of ideas for a new business website, and the distraction eased her worry over little Liam and his family. Her body jumped at the shrill sound of her phone ringing. She recognized the number, her most prominent and most anxious client Dr. Ezra Soloman, author of ten groundbreaking books on dark matter and particle physics.

"Ezra, I'm driving, so hopefully I won't lose you. Vermont has very unreliable cell service the farther north you go. How are you?" Rebecca spoke quickly to get social niceties out of the way, knowing they held little regard for Dr. Soloman.

"Rebecca, I'm reviewing the website you designed, and I'm not convinced we need all the tabs. I understand the need for the Explore and Discover tabs, but do you really think I need to have a Physics blog tab?"

"Ezra, like we've discussed, the blog is an important part of bringing in your audience. Enticing them to engage with physics more intimately. Like the beautiful meaning of your name Ezra, you're helping them to see your process, experience how your mind works in understanding the universe, and giving them, ultimately, a window into your brilliance." Rebecca heard the deep sigh escape Dr. Soloman's lips and knew she hooked him.

"Yes, yes, my brilliance, that makes sense. I'm going to send you my next article for review later today. Make sure to check your inbox. Thanks, Rebecca."

"Anytime, Ezra."

As Rebecca ended the call, she shook her head. The need for authors to be stroked, reassured, even coddled was constant. The importance of tailoring support to each individual client was an essential part of her job. She loved it all, but her favorite part was creating websites, social media platforms, trailers, marketing—that was the icing on the cake. She did it all, and she loved it all, even the constant stroking. She found it easier and safer working with words on her computer than with people. More importantly, she liked the freedom of working from home and setting her own hours.

Work was the one area of her life where she felt at peace, but lately, after watching one after another of her girlfriends in Burlington get engaged, she knew her life was missing something. Rebecca wanted to feel loved. With her long raven—sometimes unmanageable—curly hair, and big green eyes, she did have a pretty face, but she also knew she carried about twenty extra pounds. Her body was curvy and strong, at least that's what she told herself, and all the extra weight was in all the right places, but finding love eluded her.

She hoped the house would help fill the empty places inside her. Rebecca sighed as she envisioned the house that sat on a dead-end road in a small Vermont town. She knew the moment she saw the old, blue cape it would be her house. Her hidden retreat with over forty acres of land. The house was full of character, old but graceful, a home with a history. Rebecca thought of all the families before her, who had fallen in love with, lived in, and created memories in that exact house.

She made a left onto Preston Road, eyed the dead-end sign, and admired the old stone wall that ran parallel to the road. The stone was filled with granite that sparkled with the sun's kiss, giving a dignified touch to the road. *A perfect Vermont day,* she thought to herself, *with bright bluebird skies and fluffy clouds.* But in no time winter would be upon her, and Vermont winters, she knew from experience, could be brutally cold. She figured she had approximately two months to get the house in order. Her heart sped up seeing the white mailbox that still read "Parker" at the end of a long gravel driveway.

The warning bark from her dogs had her slowing down. At the edge of the woods, she glimpsed a small child, blonde hair dripping wet. Tapping the brake, again, she slowed the car more. Just as quickly, the child disappeared. She was sure the dogs sensed something too, their piercing barks still blasting her eardrums.

"Manny. Maxie! Hush!"

They obeyed. A flicker of worry crossed Rebecca's head and heart. A child. Alone. In the woods. She knew how quickly a small child could be hurt and traumatized.

Breathe. Breathe. Breathe.

"Rebecca, you're overreacting again. It's probably just a kid from the neighborhood," Jayne's steady, calm voice said in her head.

Right, just a neighbor kid taking a quick swim in the pond out back.

"Okay," she said out loud, forcing a smile. Neighbor kids playing. This is a good thing.

As she approached her house, the missing shingles on the roof stood out like a sore thumb. Oh no, shit. Did I make a mistake? She breathed through the nagging feeling of apprehension, the one that tightens the chest and wakes you up in the middle of the night. The one that comes after making life-changing decisions. *First things first. Definitely need to hire someone who can do some home repairs which won't break the bank.*

As she released the dogs from the backseat, she gazed over what she had purchased and felt a flutter in her heart—a bit of panic and a bit of excitement. She heard her dogs barking at the edge of the driveway and spied the red German luxury coupe. Definitely not a vehicle for a Vermont dirt road. The red sporty vehicle was familiar to her as it belonged to her realtor Cam Winters. Rebecca quickly glanced into the side mirror of her SUV and fixed her out of control hair.

Chapter 3

Cam Winters had a million-dollar smile, wavy sandy-brown hair, and the deepest blue eyes she had ever seen. All six-foot-three of him screamed male, and with the successful-sexy vibe, the combination was hard to resist. Rebecca recalled the day she met Cam—his smile drew her in, but even better were his eyes. Piercing eyes so powerful that they knocked her slightly off-balance. The first meeting with Cam, she lost her voice when he entered the room. His penetrating gaze tore through her soul, made her feel naked, exposed, and left her weak in the knees. Completely off-kilter, she'd forgotten why she'd been standing in his office in the first place. Remembering that day had her blushing. *Great, get a grip, girl.*

Cam eased out of the car, stirring up all kinds of nice and naughty thoughts in her. Focus, Rebecca, focus, she told herself. Her chest constricted slightly as he bent to retrieve something from the backseat. She waved to him as he sauntered up the driveway. Every inch of him strutting, perfectly tailored in a suit the color of his eyes, and she felt her blush deepen. Did she imagine it? Or was he moving in slow motion? Every single muscle seemed to throb as he walked. He was hot, model hot, and something in Rebecca's thought, said he knew it.

"Rebecca," Cam spoke her name and broke the

spell she was under. She met his crystal blue eyes.

"Where'd you go?" he asked as he lazily dragged a hand through his sandy-brown hair.

"Sorry, sorry, I was thinking about repairs."

"Oh yeah, well, now you understand why the property was such a good deal."

"I suppose."

"Don't worry. I know a guy, Jack Corcoran, he's solid."

"And, hopefully, reasonable."

"Don't you worry, I will send him over. I came by with the final deed, which outlines the property, forty acres plus or minus."

He reached into the leather briefcase, collected the paperwork, and aligned his body close to hers so she could read. It was then she got a whiff of his cologne— the heady male scent that had her imagining her body with his. Yet a voice in her head was nagging at her to be careful. *Could he be the guy? He could be for tonight.*

After Cam left, with everything signed, sealed, and neatly placed in his briefcase, she took the keys he'd handed her and opened the door. *Home.* With the dogs on her heels, she entered. After releasing Lulu from the cat carrier, with hands on hips, she studied the large living room and imagined the room with fresh coats of paint in colors of soft blues and yellows. Her furniture, covered with pillows and soft throws, would be neatly arranged in front of the wood stove, the large cape windows covered in sheer pastel drapes allowing the sun rays in. Candles, flowers, paintings, and, most important, her family photos hung on the walls. *Home.*

Chapter 4

Jack Corcoran was pissed! The plumber was supposed to be here at 7 a.m. sharp, and now it was quarter past noon. *What the fuck?* At this rate, the job would be, at least, two weeks behind, and the owner, Cal Anderson, would be chewing out his ass because of it. Usually, Jack loved the responsibility of being the lead contractor on a job. But the position came with its fair share of headaches, and Cal Anderson and the late plumber would be major ones. *What the hell!*

From his estimate, the whole house needed new piping throughout. As Jack waited, his dog, Keeper, an Irish Wolfhound, kept watch staring out the front window. While Jack waited, he scribbled the pros and cons of going with PEX versus copper. He knew the cost would be a significant factor for the homeowner and always dreaded the conversation about quality over price.

Jack was a man who, like his father, was a bit headstrong but quiet, especially with feelings of the heart. He'd rather work with his hands. Less talk, more doing. Yet he was determined to get what he wanted and wasn't scared to work for it. Jack had two soft spots—dogs and babies—both made him smile with pleasure, and both he would rather hang out with than most adults. With dogs and babies, there were no hidden agendas.

He also realized his life was missing something, but that something was hard to find, and he'd tried, especially taking a couple of rounds between the sheets with Melanie, the local bartender from the next town over. Melanie was good company on a cold night, plenty of spark between the sheets, and there was many a cold night in Vermont, but there'd been no spark in the heart. And Jack knew he needed more than a good lay. *No,* Jack thought, *I want more than just a good lay,* especially after losing his first real love, Alice, to another man. A betrayal that still stung.

Jack thought of his parents, Henry and Millie, who would soon be celebrating their fortieth wedding anniversary. He wanted what his parents had, the whole package. A companion who warmed the night but also warmed the heart. A partner for the long haul who would hold his hand and stand by him during tough times and who would be there to celebrate the good.

Someday, Jack thought, *someday.* He was startled out of his head by the sound of his phone. He recognized the number—Cal Anderson, the owner of the current remodel.

"Cal, what can I do you for?"

"Well, Jack, I'm just calling to check on the status. The missus is threatening to divorce me if I can't give her a firm date on when we can move in. Actually, on second thought, the divorce might be welcomed," Cal said snorting. "All kidding aside Jack, what do you have for me?"

"Cal, you know it's impossible to give you a firm date. I'm doing my best, but we ran into some unforeseen issues with the plumbing. Since I have you on the phone, it might be a good time to talk about the budget."

"Jack, how many times do I have to say it, there's no wiggle room in the budget. I thought we settled this already."

"Yes, we did, Cal, but if you want running water and a flushing toilet, we need to talk. The whole system needs to be replaced. You can go with copper piping, which is dependable but costly. I want you to consider going with PEX, a third the cost of copper."

"You're talking Greek to me, Jack, again, there's *no* room in the budget. Figure it out, Jack, that's what I'm paying you for." Jack heard the click and the steam coming through the phone.

"Fuck," Jack cursed as he heard the loud knock at the front door. *Finally*, he thought, *if I'm getting chewed out, so are you*. He took the stairs two at a time and threw open the front door and bellowed. "Where the hell have you been?"

Jack was surprised and a bit irritated to be met by Camden Winters, Eden's local realtor, better known in these parts as "Cam the Sham."

There was a time when Jack had trusted Cam with his life. They'd met in kindergarten, and Jack had immediately known that Cam needed a friend. Cam was like a dog kicked too many times, slow to warm up and distrustful. Jack had gone out of his way to get Cam to trust him, and soon they were inseparable brothers. But that all changed two years ago when Jack found Cam in bed with his girlfriend, Alice.

"Hey Jack," Cam said tensely.

"What do you want?" Jack said impatiently, thrusting his hands in his pockets and leaning his tall frame against the kitchen counter.

"Well, you know I sold the Parker place on Preston."

"Yep, I heard you found a city dweller. Surprised it sold. The listing was outrageous for this area."

"Yeah, well, you would be surprised what people don't know, especially flat-landers."

"I imagine honesty gets in the way of a big fat commission," he said, sounding more righteous than he meant to.

"Ouch, Jack, and for the record, I don't give a rat's ass what you think of my business practices." Cam smoothed the expensive fabric of his tailored blue sport coat and shifted to check out his image in the mirror.

Jack thought of Alice. His Alice, who was sweet and innocent. Unaware that men could be pigs. Trusting when the best friend of her current boyfriend told her she was settling. That she could do better than Jack. Making Alice question that she needed a man who was more refined. Jack still felt the sucker punch to his gut. *Two years ago. Not long enough to forget.* Jack hadn't seen it coming. Jack did see his best friend growing cockier by the minute with each sale, with each conquest, with each new sports car, but he'd never imagined his best friend would seduce his girlfriend. *Boy, did I learn the hard way.*

"No, Cam, I'm upset over you taking advantage of people, good, hardworking people." Jack could feel the anger building.

"I'm not here to rehash the past, Jack, or like you said, take advantage," Cam said, while smoothing his hair in the mirror.

"What happened to you? You turned into such an asshole." Jack narrowed his eyes at Cam.

"Ouch, again, Jack, I'm deeply wounded," Cam said, sarcastically putting his hand to his heart. "I'm here because the lady who bought the cape needs some repairs done before it turns cold. And, naturally, I thought of you."

"You, naturally, thought of me? Why? Oh, let me think, hmm, guilt, maybe? No wait, I see, you know I will do right by her. When she realizes she has been scammed, you expect me to swoop in and smooth things over. Give her a deal on the repairs, perhaps, clean up after you because that's what I do."

"You've always been a good boy scout, Jack."

"Because I care about the reputation of this town, and I don't like honest, hardworking people being taken advantage of. The shit you do, Cam, tarnishes all of us."

"Well, there's that. Truth be told, Jack, I did feel my balls grow a little bigger with the sale of that old cape." He said, cupping his balls and smirking.

Jack felt his body tense, his heart pumping wildly. He pushed forward off the counter, adrenaline coursing through his body. He fought the urge to wipe the pretentious smirk off Cam's face. He needed the satisfaction of pummeling him, for Alice, for himself, for taking away his dream, for what was lost and what could've been.

"Control yourself, Jack. I told the new owner you'd be coming by. We both know Corcoran and Sons needs the work."

"Don't worry Cam, I'll swing by, not because of you, but yes, Corcoran and Sons could use the work. But this doesn't fix things between us. There is no fixing for what you did. You have to live with that and live with yourself," he said.

"Always a pleasure, Jack," Cam said.

"Right back at you, Cam." Jack slammed the door behind him. "Fuckin' prick," he screamed, thoroughly pissed. He paced the length of the room and raised a fist to hit the wall and stopped himself. There was no denying that Corcoran and Sons needed the work, which stung all the more, especially knowing that the work came from Cam. The past year had been a rough year all around for business, so he'd take the job. It was a hard pill to swallow to accept work from Cam. Being in the same room with him, the man who single-handedly ended his relationship with the woman he planned to marry, made all the hurt and anger come flooding back. Knowing there was little he could do, Jack stormed out of the house and walked it off.

Chapter 5

The notification on her cellphone told her the moving truck's ETA was approximately forty-five minutes. She was ready to get the day going and get her house in order. Last night she made a makeshift bed— an old sleeping bag and a pillow from the trunk of her car. Rebecca stretched out on the living room floor with her two dogs right beside her. As she drifted to sleep, she listened to the night sounds and delighted in the way the moon shined into the living room, the soft glow placing a charming touch on her furnishings.

The sounds of summer brought a peaceful presence to the old cape, with the windows wide open welcoming the chirp of crickets, the wind as it rustled through the leaves, and a stray owl's hoot. All night sounds that lulled Rebecca under its song into a deep sleep. She slept that first night soundly and woke up late, out of a dream. Hands stretched above her head, Rebecca felt the stiffness in her lower back release some. She worked to crack the kinks out and stretched some more. More of the dream took hold. She closed her eyes and quieted her mind to let the dream come forward.

In the dream, Camden Winters stood next to her in a meadow. His clothes dripped with water. A tall man dressed in all black passed them. He held the hand of a small child, a little girl with long blonde hair. The child was humming, skipping alongside the man in black as they walked. A smile widened on the little girl's face as they walked toward a blue pool of water in the middle of the meadow. The man in black pulled at the little girl's arm, cursed her for walking slow, and screamed for her to move faster. The girl's face filled with worry. She looked back at Rebecca with eyes spilling with tears and mouthed, "Help me." Cam turned to Rebecca in the dream and whispered, "Run."

Rebecca thought of the little blonde girl she spied yesterday and grabbed her cellphone. The glimpse of the child as she drove up, the one who stood at the edge of the woods. Her chest tightened as the little girl's image became more ominous. She pulled up Murphy's contact in her phone. "Murphy, call Captain Murphy, he'll make it better," she said to herself. He picked up on the first ring.

"Becca, I wondered when I'd hear from you again. It's been six months."

"Captain Murphy, you do know you're the only one I let get away with calling me, Becca besides family." She smiled at his use of her pet name, one he picked up from her parents all those years ago. It took her back to the day. The day she remembered clearly as it was yesterday when a then-young Detective Murphy, a Boston beat cop from her neighborhood, sat in her hospital room and made her feel smart. With a notebook in hand, the young cop frantically wrote down everything her little seven-year-old mind saw and felt. He never once questioned her, never once looked at her funny or called her a liar. Rebecca trusted him, so she told him everything about the little girl named Allison who was being held captive.

The sound of his voice jolted her out of the memory.

"That's why it's so special for me to call you Becca. After all these years I feel like family. How are you?"

"I just moved," she replied.

"Away from Burlington? I'm surprised. I thought you loved it."

"I did, I do, but it was becoming too big, too noisy. You know," she said.

"I completely understand," he said. "Remember it's important that I have a current address on file for you."

"Yes, I know the routine," she said. Rebecca smiled visualizing Murphy's serious face.

"Are you happy?" he asked quietly.

"Yes, well, I think so. I had a dream last night." She heard the concerned sigh as he exhaled.

"You don't have to worry, Becca. He's still locked up. If anything changes, you know you'd be the first I'd call," he said.

"I know but, well, I don't have to tell you…"

"Your dreams are important. I do know. I hear from Allison every month. She often asks about you, wondering how you're doing, and always expresses her gratitude. You know if it wasn't for your bravery she wouldn't be here today."

"Is she doing well?"

"Yes, she was just accepted into medical school. She's very excited. Wants to be a pediatrician."

"Well, Murphy, we both have you to thank. We both know not too many adults respect or take seriously what children have to say. I'll always be thankful you listened to me."

"You know I'm always here if you need to talk. I'm still a good listener. That will never change, remember, anytime you need to talk. Also, I want to hear if you have more dreams."

"You'll be the first to know. Thanks, Murphy."

Sure, Murphy was right, her perpetrator was locked up, but that didn't mean he still wasn't coming for her. After he was sentenced and put away, she was terrified of the night and often spent it wide awake staring at her bedroom window instead of sleeping. Waiting for him to find her, and there were nights he did find her. In her dreams, he'd come for her, and it was in those dreams she'd have to outsmart him all over again.

Initially, her mother would sleep with her after she woke up screaming from a dream, her mother cooing to her that she was home and safe. Rebecca could still hear her mother's voice in her head and feel her arms around her. *Sshh, lamby, Mama has you, you're safe.* She learned from an early age it was far more complicated than that. Rebecca was never really safe; in her dreams, he made it clear to her that he was still out there. When she started therapy with Jayne and shared her nightmares, Rebecca learned all about psychic dreaming. Jayne taught her how to protect herself at night so that her abuser could no longer terrorize her while she slept and dreamed.

Hanging up with Murphy, she checked the time on her phone. She wondered if she had time to get a much-needed cup of coffee at the local gas station before the moving truck arrived. The dogs flew into a frenzy hearing the large truck hit a rut in the road. Rebecca jumped up, her dogs following in pursuit as she ran to the window to check it out. She listened to the moving truck's loud whine as it backed up into her driveway.

It was time to claim her new life, time to make her home a home. She patted the heads of her two pups and opened the door. "Coffee is going to have to wait."

****

He stopped and parked the old truck down the road, climbed out, and cut his way through the woods. He knew he had to be careful, couldn't risk being caught, like all the times before. He had it down to a science—leave no trace behind and let no one see you. He knew where to park, how not to draw attention or suspicion. He knew how to cover his tracks.

As he waited for the moving truck to leave, he took stock of the old house and its new occupant. A pretty little thing. As he watched her, he felt his erection grow, and he praised God when the movers finally left. He preferred having her to himself without the distraction of the other men around. He'd stalked plenty of young women over the years, but this one was special. He liked the way her body strained as she bent over to pick up a box, how the fabric of her jeans pulled tightly over her ass, exposing more of her to him—his own private show.

He watched as she lifted the back of her hand to wipe the sweat that had formed on her brow and fantasized about making her whole body sweat. As he touched himself, he closed his eyes, imagined her slowly removing her clothing, piece by piece, giving his tongue access to all that luscious sweat trickling down her body. His tongue exploring all of her as she strained under him, fighting, liking it rough. As he sat in the woods, camouflaged by the cedar trees, he licked his hand as he rubbed himself harder. He knew how to stay downwind so his scent would not be detected. He laughed to himself that he had outwitted her dogs, who were busy marking their territory.

He noticed her skittishness, the way she lifted her head to look around from time to time, knowing she sensed him, his prey. It aroused him even more, similar to a deer caught in his crosshairs not knowing which way he would strike, or when he would pull the trigger. He felt damn lucky, damn surprised, to have found such a fine piece when he came back to check on the family homestead. He thought he'd see another young family move in. Jesus, the last family had a boatload of brats running around and stayed in the house forever, but he always kept watch. Yes, he thought, he was going to enjoy keeping watch on this young thing. *After all, someone has to mind the store.*

Chapter 6

Jack was angry with himself for agreeing to swing by the old Parker place. Corcoran and Sons did need the work, but he hated the fact he was doing Cam a favor. As Jack drove through the town he grew up in and loved, thoughts of Alice filled his head. He replayed the endless talks of planning their future together, buying land, building a house, getting married, having a bunch of kids. All talk from young lovers who dream of playing house. All talk that went out the window when Alice admitted her love for Cam and her plan to marry his best friend. All plans that Cam had no intention of following through with, because he'd only wanted Alice naked and vulnerable. Just the way Cam liked his women.

Inwardly, Jack felt the hurt, knew the exact location where it squeezed his heart. He could never forgive Cam for stealing the love of his life. Jack would never forgive Alice's betrayal, either. Two people he gave his heart to, two people he trusted with his life, one his blood brother, and the other the woman he'd planned on marrying.

He thought of the quote from his favorite movie, *"sometimes you eat the bear, and sometimes the bear eats you."* Well, he was done with the past, done dwelling in the hate, and it was time for Jack to make peace with the bear.

He turned on the dead-end road, stopped, and stared at the old Parker place. *Yup, it needs work.* The landscape alone was out of control. He would need to bring his tractor and start cleaning it up.

His eyes started on the roof. He predicted at least thirty years old. It was missing some shingles, but the water stains concerned him more. Best to go with a standing seam—costly, but, in the end, a money saver. His eyes traveled down the wooden planks to the chimney. Foundation cracks need to be sealed up. *Jesus,* he thought to himself, *I'm not even out of my truck yet.* He did love the old cape with its wooden frame, classic central door, and pitched roof. With all its beautiful New England character, he cursed Cam who'd clearly taken advantage of the poor sucker who bought the house. Jack would inspect the whole house from top to bottom. Make sure to provide a thorough list of what really needed tending. There was something about the house beyond its history that pulled him to the project. Yes, Corcoran and Sons did need the work, but not that bad. The old house was special and a part of the history of Eden. He just hoped the new owner felt the same way.

Jack eased himself out of his pickup and grabbed his notebook and pencil. As he walked to the front, he noted the stairs leading to the beautiful central front door were crooked and the railing needed some tending to. He started jotting down notes, ideas, costs as he slowly made his way around the side of the house. He hunched down to inspect the foundation. The house was leaning to one side, and he worried about the significant cracks along the foundation just possibly contributing to a structural issue. As he rose to his feet, his eyes followed the lines of the house. Yup, he thought, the old cape needed much more than just a new paint job.

He started to mutter to himself as he wrote in his notebook, then heard the flapping wings of a grouse taking flight in the distance. Following the sound, he gazed out to the field on the west side of the property and saw a woman with long, dark, curly hair gingerly walk across the tall grass with two husky German shepherds. Her long hair blowing in the wind, at her feet the two dogs sniffed out what he thought might be a rabbit or possibly turkeys. The woman had a hell of a smile on her face and, he didn't mind saying, a hell of a body. She wore torn jeans and a snug red flannel shirt. She seemed happy walking in the tall grass. He noticed when she jumped suddenly, startled by something, probably a garter snake in the grass. The surprise in the grass had her clutching her heart, and she laughed at herself, which made him smile. It had been a long time since he'd witnessed anyone this happy, this relaxed and at peace in nature. He realized that he missed that feeling, that feeling of joy and being content.

With efficiency, she called to the dogs who raised their heads and came running to her. Jack watched as they sniffed the air, gave out a warning bark, growled, and fixated on him. The woman turned, shaded her eyes from the sun to get a better view, and gave a command to her dogs. They stopped the low growl immediately but walked protectively in front of her as she headed back to the house. She smiled as she approached him, let her dogs sniff at his feet, and said, "Hello. Can I help you?"

He paused for a moment and took her all in. First, he noticed the intense green eyes with the thick dark lashes, the smattering of freckles on her nose, the one dimple on the right side of her full mouth that appeared when she smiled. *Heart-stopping beautiful. Isn't there an Irish jig about a green-eyed girl? There should be about this one,* Jack thought, and it all began with a simple hello.

Chapter 7

"I'm Jack. Jack Corcoran. Cam Winters asked me to stop by to look over the repairs." Jack extended his hand. Rebecca hesitated, noticing the strong forearm, and, placing her hand in his, welcomed the warm, firm grip of his handshake. She met his eyes and studied him noting that this man before her was ridiculously hot. Jack Corcoran was lanky but buff, with soft brown eyes and dark wavy hair. He wore the hair a little too long, definitely could use a haircut. She estimated him to be in his early thirties. With his broad chest, rugged clothes, and driving a black super-duty pickup she figured, if the commercials were right, he was single. *God, she hoped so.*

"Yes, of course, thank you for coming. Cam mentioned he knew a guy. I'm Rebecca McCabe."

He nodded politely and grinned. "Nice to meet you, Rebecca McCabe, welcome to Eden. It looks like I caught you unloading." He pointed to the boxes on the ground before handing her his business card.

Her face heated as she blushed. She took a glance at his card to give herself a minute. *Jesus,* she thought, *can I have a little self-control here? Pull it together.*

"I was retrieving some things from the car earlier. Most of the boxes are inside. I decided to take the dogs for a quick walk and explore the grounds."

"Is this a bad time?" he asked.

"No, no, not at all! Truthfully, I'm anxious to get the house in order."

"McCabe sounds Irish," Jack said.

"Yes, Boston Irish." Rebecca turned to face him and nodded. "I noticed your card says, Corcoran and Sons. You have sons?"

He laughed, and she noticed his eyes twinkled with the laughter.

"I'm one of the sons. I took over the family contracting business from my semi-retired father, Henry Corcoran. Although I'm not sure he'll ever fully retire."

"Corcoran also sounds Irish," Rebecca said as she met his eyes.

"I won't deny it. What brings you to Eden, Rebecca?"

She took her time, gathering her words carefully.

"I just needed a quieter place to think. Sometimes, in a city, it's impossible to think, too much noise, too many people," she mused.

"Couldn't agree more."

Rebecca stopped herself from telling the rest, learning not to share her life story too quickly. She stooped to pick at a couple of wild daisies in the grass. "Anyway, I see you have a notebook. I've been making some notes of my own. Maybe we should start by comparing notes?"

"Sounds good."

"Come on in. Just to warn you, there are boxes everywhere. I'm still unpacking."

Jack followed Rebecca up the front steps. The two German shepherds moved in before him, edging him out of the way, and practically off the front steps. He laughed at the two dogs as they made their way into the house. Motioning to the dogs, Rebecca explained, "They tend to be a tad bit protective of me, very insistent on following me everywhere I go. I call them my velcro pups." As she spoke, tails hit the floor thumping loudly. Jack moved to stroke the head of the nearest German shepherd, and the dog's body went crazy with excitement.

"Manny likes you; the other is Max. Do you have dogs?"

"I have one, Keeper, an Irish Wolfhound. He's a great dog but not a great listener. He lets his nose rule his body and his brain, but these dogs are seriously nice dogs, really well behaved." He met Rebecca's eyes and smiled.

As she closed the door behind them, a loud creak from the hinges caused her to startle. "I'm not used to that sound yet. I guess that should be added to the list." The look in his eyes made her wonder if he was surveying the room—seeing all the boxes and furniture in disarray. "I know, I know, I have a lot of unpacking to do." Rebecca sighed and continued, "I never realized buying a house entailed so much work. It seems never-ending."

"No worries, it will all come together in time." He rapped his knuckles on the wall. "This house has really good bones. The previous owners, the Parkers, hosted the best parties in this house. The whole town would show up. They always made the house stand out, lights everywhere, candles, decorations. It really shined."

Rebecca beamed as she listened to the story and wondered if he was trying to calm her nerves. *He's sweet,* she thought to herself. "I fell in love with this house as soon as I saw it. In fact, I fell in love with the road driving up. Eden is a beautiful place," she said, her green eyes honed in on his brown, and they both held the stare.

She watched as he took a tape measure out of his back pocket and measured and marked the wall.

"No argument, Eden is special." Jack stopped what he was doing. "I've lived here my whole life, and I don't think a day goes by that I don't feel lucky," he said, glancing back at her.

The intensity in his brown eyes made her heart soften. "Umm, I think I left my notebook in the kitchen. I'll be right back," she said, walking quickly to the kitchen. She stopped herself and turned back. "Wait, I forgot my manners. Can I get you anything?"

"All set, thanks," Jack replied as he busied himself checking the flue on the stove.

Standing in the kitchen, she muttered to herself as she placed dishes in the sink. "Relax, relax. Yes, he's cute, seriously jacked, and super sweet, but you know nothing about him. I wonder if it's too early for a drink?" *Yes, way too early,* she thought. *Come on, woman up.*

She came back into the living room to find him bent over the wood stove inspecting the venting system. Rebecca felt her face flush, once again, as she took in all of Jack's body—well, specifically, all of his backside, which was firm and tight. *Ahh, a man's butt in jeans, a thing of beauty.* Rebecca needed her cellphone to take a quick photo and talk over the perfection of his butt with her friends, preferably over a glass of wine. She stifled a laugh and wondered, was it wrong to take a photo of a complete stranger's butt to place on the internet? One she just met? She would make a note to check her calendar and arrange a girl's night out soon with her Burlington girlfriends. As she lingered watching his butt move in his jeans, she was leaning on the side of, yes, most definitely a photo.

Rebecca coughed to get Jack's attention. He turned to see her in the doorway, clutching the notebook in her hand. She started in on the list. "So—some shingles need replacing on the roof, chimney patching, some floor sanding throughout the house. I would love to bring back these old pine floors. I just want them to stand out. I noticed the water throughout the house runs brown, not sure what it means or if it will clear up with time. A new kitchen sink needs to be installed. I'm thinking one of those farmhouse sinks. Also, I would love a new tub in the upstairs bathroom; a good soaking tub is essential for this house and for me. I don't think I can make it through the winter without a good tub, you know one of those deep tubs with jets; the one upstairs is super old."

She stopped talking when he cleared his throat. She was all but certain it was his way to interrupt her. Without hesitation, he flipped open his notebook and started in. "The roof needs to be replaced. Professionally speaking, I would go with a standing seam. Costly, but you save the money in longevity. After the roof, I would tackle the chimney repair. You need to have it inspected, cleaned, the whole nine yards, make sure once fall's here it's in working order. The foundation cracks need to be sealed, but before any foundation work, I want my team to check out the structural soundness of the whole house. I don't know if you've noticed, but the house slants, your front steps are leaning, and the railing is loose."

Rebecca followed his eyes to the ceiling as he pointed with his pencil to a cluster of crescent-shaped stains.

"What you have here, I'm afraid, is water damage—most likely a leak coming from your upstairs bathroom. I wouldn't be taking any long showers for a while," he said with a wink. "Next the yard—you have major landscaping needs. Given this house sat empty for over a year, you should think about inspecting for rodents, especially in the cellar. I don't have to tell you, but rats are prolific breeders. They're not big on birth control," he joked. "The house needs a paint job, but that could wait until next year. I am concerned about lead in the paint. You should think about getting it tested given the age of the house. I will need time to inspect the interior when…"

She saw his mouth moving, but her mind couldn't catch up with his words. She bent over with perspiration pooling in her armpits, rested her hands on her knees, and tried to catch her breath.

"Hey, hey, what's going on? Are you okay?" he asked.

"I need to sit."

She let him take her arm as he helped her to the couch.

"Sit, sit, come on now, Rebecca, just sit down. Are you okay?"

For a split second, she fell back against the couch cushions and closed her eyes. Bolting forward, she placed her head between her knees and gasped. "I'm, I'm fine, I just need to breathe. I can't breathe lying back."

"Okay," Jack said.

"Is it hot in here? It is hot in here! I can't breathe." She collapsed farther forward. "I'm freaking out. Your list, your list, the money. Rats! Prolific breeders! Seriously!" Rebecca gasped. "Am I a moron? Why would I buy such a house? I am a moron. How could I let myself be such a moron? No, no, no, I love this house. It really wasn't an impulsive decision. I swear. I do love it. I think I'm having a heart attack. Can you open a window?" She moaned, rubbing a hand to her chest. Her dog, Max, sat at her side panting as he pawed at her pant leg, while Manny paced the length of the room, back and forth. Lulu sat in the window watching the commotion.

"Rebecca, look at me, just breathe, slow, slow— good." She stared into his eyes and felt their warmth steady her. As she breathed, he breathed with her, and the beating of her heart slowed.

"There you go. In and out. In and out. Good, good," he soothed.

"I'm good. I'm okay. I love this house."

"Good, good, there you go, nice and easy," Jack said, his hand on her back. "It's going to be okay."

Listening to his voice, she believed him. "Yes, it will be. I'm okay now."

"Let me get you some water." Rebecca motioned to the kitchen.

"Here you go," he said as he unscrewed the top and waited for her to take the water.

"Thanks, just a bit of panic. I'm really okay," she said. As she took the bottle from him, his fingers touched hers, and she could've sworn she felt a spark.

"Great kitchen, by the way," he gestured toward

the kitchen.

"It really is, isn't it?

He gave her a reassuring nod. "And if I'm not mistaken, that's the original crown molding in the living room." He sat down next to her and pointed out the molding above. "Beautiful, you just don't see craftsmanship like that anymore."

Rebecca's eyes followed Jack's and smiled taking in the beautiful etched molding.

"Thank you, Jack."

"No worries, okay?" Jack asked softly, squeezing her knee in comfort.

Rebecca took a big breath and said, "No worries."

Chapter 8

After what seemed like forever, Rebecca finally had her house in order. She'd unpacked more boxes than she cared to remember. Parts of her body ached in places she didn't know existed. She cursed out loud as she lowered herself to the toilet and wondered to herself if she was too young to have a bar installed. She ached from top to bottom. *Oh well,* she thought to herself, *at least I got a workout in.* Even knowing there was a laundry list of repairs that needed tending to, it didn't change her mind. The house was perfect, needed repairs and all.

In a lot of ways she was like the house—at one point she needed to be put back together and like her house, knew it was a process. She felt at home. She knew there was a story somewhere about this house, and she wanted to find out what it was. At night, she swore she heard a woman crying, and oddly, a child giggling. And this morning she'd swear something stroked her hair and woke her from a sound sleep. Maybe it was just her imagination getting the better of her but then again maybe not. She'd make a plan to go to the local library, perhaps the town clerk's office, and do some research.

She turned to her pups. "Doesn't every old house have spirits?" The two German shepherds curled up in their dog beds, one softly snoring, the other barely lifting his head to acknowledge that she spoke. "Come on, guys, not even a thump of the tail?" She grabbed her coffee, sipped, and leaned back in her favorite chair. In her experience, it took a while to become used to a new place, but as she took in the room, she felt like she'd always belonged to this house.

A sense of contentment settled in her body as she let her eyes wander over the touches she added. Wild daisies, freshly picked from the field, filled the crystal vase that sat on the antique marble table, a gift from her favorite aunt. Photos of her family, human, canine, and feline were scattered around the room. Dried wood sat stacked in the steel grate next to the wood stove. Her soft cashmere throws in colors of soft ivory draped over the couch and chairs, all just waiting for the first bite of cold air in the wind.

"It does feel like home," she said to her sleeping pups.

She walked to the window, spied a red cardinal scoop seed from the birdfeeder in the apple tree out front. She envisioned the months ahead sitting at her desk, looking out the window, watching the snow fall. The scene was perfect, except for one thing, and with this thought, Rebecca felt the ache in her heart. All of her life she was told, soon it would be her turn, there's a pot for every lid, her mother would say. Rebecca had heard it all, but her heart was lonely today.

Her cat, Lulu, weaved in and around her legs, rubbing her back against Rebecca's leg for comfort. She reached down to pet Lulu's head. She yelled out to her pups in the living room, "Let's get your collars on and go for a walk." She grabbed a light sweater off the back of the chair.

As Rebecca entered the kitchen, Manny and Max were already turning in excited circles. Maxie dropped on his belly, crawling in anticipation across the floor. She attached the collars and smiled. Look for the beauty, she reminded herself, opened the door, and said, "Let's go, guys."

She headed down the path toward the pond, feeling the rush of cold air hit her body, and instinctually pulled the sweater about her. Strange, she thought, as an image appeared in front of her eyes. A little girl skipping, holding someone's hand—the image from her dream. As she tried to focus, the image slithered away, replaced by another, this time, one of a man, lying in wait. Maybe a hunter, she thought.

"Rebecca," she heard a woman's voice call her name, like a whisper on the wind. She turned in the direction of the sound. *Odd,* she thought to herself, as the wind picked up again and a chill made its way down her spine. *Maybe just the wind playing tricks on me.*

"Okay, guys, a couple of tennis balls in the pond and then back to work." With her okay, Max and Manny ran ahead of her.

Reaching the pond, she stopped, enchanted by the water's bluish-green color. The hues of the water richly dotted with lily pads waiting for wildlife to hold. She heard her mother's encouraging voice in her head, "you found the beauty, that's my girl, nice work." Indeed, she had, and she physically felt her soul lighten as she took in the tranquil beauty. As she stood at the pond's edge the tranquility was replaced with a warning that had the hairs on the back of her neck standing up. *Take heed, or you'll be next.*

****

As the tree stand swayed in the large maple, a droplet of water from a leaf above him hit his right cheek. He braced his body, legs spread evenly to balance as he sat firmly on the seat. He checked the full-body harness, pulled the strap tighter, and thought to himself, uncomfortable but safe. What was the saying, "an ounce of prevention is worth a pound of cure?" He leaned down and picked up his thermos. He sipped the tepid coffee and checked his watch for the time, three hours in and waiting. Years of hunting had taught him the importance of patience. There was no rushing while stalking prey. You had to sit, bide your time, and wait. *And wait.*

He bit his lower lip as he heard them approach. His body trembled slightly, eager with anticipation and need. The adrenaline surged through his body. He lived for the feeling—the addiction to an adrenaline rush was better than any drug on the street. It was time. His stand was set with optimal shooting lanes in which to aim. He knew he had a clean shot. With his tripod set, he aimed and clicked. Photo after photo. He knew the importance of manipulating the habitat to capture his game. Spreading deer urine along the bank was a genius move. He knew it would throw off his scent and improve his chances of going undetected and capturing her.

****

Max and Manny sat, eyes glued to the tennis ball in her hand. From the grass, Rebecca followed her pups' path, who were in a fast chase, and laughed as Manny pounced, missed, ending with Maxie nabbing the ball. "Better luck next time, Buddy," she said as she patted Manny's head and headed to the pond's bank. The dogs stopped suddenly, nose to the ground, whimpered, and paced the bank's perimeter—back and forth in confused circles. Above her head, two black crows swooped down off the large maple tree planted at the edge and circled overhead. Both birds cawed, the shadow of their wings falling across her face. *An omen.*

She quickly attached the lead to her dogs' collars as they started to bark with increasing fervor. When she placed her hand out, both dogs crouched down in submission. She knew this was their sign for fear, but for the life of her she couldn't figure out what had them scared. The warning replayed in her head—*take heed, or you'll be next.*

A pungent odor hit her nostrils as she knelt in front of Max and Manny. "Hey, hey, hey, what's up with you two? What's got you spooked? Deer? Turkeys? Did turkeys come through here?" With a soothing voice, she rubbed her hands down the lengths of them to stop their quivering. She searched the ground for tracks and any signs of trouble, coyote, fisher, maybe deer. She gripped the lead firmly in her hand and braced her body just in case they spied the culprit causing the uproar.

She paused to listen, hearing only the wind rustling in the leaves, and shivered. She quickly buttoned up her sweater as the sun peeked out from behind a cloud. Rebecca followed the sun's path as it drifted lazily over the pond's surface. She touched the bark of a large maple tree at the pond's edge and thought about how everything in nature had a presence. Here, at the pond, she felt a steady pulse, intense at times. One her dogs were sensing, and one, today, that did not feel altogether benevolent.

She led her dogs to the knoll and sat, welcoming

the sun's rays as they warmed her face and body. Putting her face up to the sun, she closed her eyes for a brief moment. Still, the feeling of unease remained. A picture formed in her mind—a man with a camera. A seatbelt covered his body. She tried to focus her energy on his face, but it remained hidden. Frustrated, she gave up and walked her dogs home.

****

He'd watched her through the lens. Her large breasts bouncing, her thighs straining as she bent over to calm her stupid dogs. The perfect trap.

"Dumb fucking dogs," he said with a snicker.

With each click, his need grew stronger, the craving building in his veins. He stopped, laid his head back against the tree, and stalked her only with his eyes as she sunned herself on the grass. His fantasy was building—her hand reaching down to unzip him and release him. On her knees, in front of him as he guided her mouth to taste, to suck. Forcing his prey to take him in deeper. He stifled his groan as he released.

Chapter 9

Having finished his meal at the Coffee Corner, Cam sat in the booth alone. He gave a sly smile to the beautiful blonde with her husband sitting in the booth across from him. He tracked her movement as she crossed and uncrossed her legs seductively, giving him a peek. The blonde's husband sat across from her, playing on his cellphone, oblivious as the two of them danced.

Cam loved the game. He considered his ability to make women want him an art form. Getting them hot and squirming with desire was the ultimate ego-booster. And most of all, he loved walking away while they pondered what was wrong with them when he withdrew his attention. He waited for his check and smirked at his finesse for making this particular blonde respond so quickly. So quickly, in fact, it bored him, and he lost interest.

He eyed Jack at the counter ordering. *Smug bastard*. Cam hated to admit that what Jack had said the other day pissed him off. In his heart, he knew Jack saw through him. Cam pulled himself to his feet, threw a couple of dollars on the table before grabbing the check. He gave the blonde a wink as he passed her table and eased up to the counter with the check in hand.

"Jack."

Catching Jack's eye, Cam saw it, the look of

contempt.

"Cam," he said flatly, turning back toward the clerk at the counter. "Thanks, Bonnie."

"You're welcome, Jack. I put some extra bacon on it for you. I know how much you like bacon."

"You're a sweetheart. Thank you. Have a good day."

Cam stepped to the side as Jack gathered up his coffee and breakfast sandwich from the counter. He watched as the clerk batted her eyelashes at Jack.

It pissed Cam off to see a woman flirt with Jack. *What a waste*. Cam knew he was better than Jack in every way. Time to prove it.

"Bonnie, honey, is that a new haircut?" Cam said with a seductive wink. With eyes cast down, Cam slowly followed the length of her body, inch by inch. His big finish—a seductive smile that conveyed, "Wanna fuck!" It never failed.

"I had it done a couple of days ago, thanks for noticing. How've you…"

He turned and walked away.

"Thanks again, Bonnie. And the hair does look nice," said Jack.

Outside, Cam heard the footsteps behind him and felt Jack's push from behind. *Bingo*.

"Why are you such a major prick? What do you need to prove?"

"Who, me? Nothing. What's got your undies in a bunch, Jack?" Cam gave Jack a shit-eating grin. "Just appreciating a lady's new look. Can't I notice a beautiful woman without being called a prick?"

With a sharp, angry stride, Jack shouldered past Cam on the way to his truck.

"That's what I thought, Jack, once a pussy, always a pussy."

****

Jack set his coffee down on the cab of his truck. Anger coursing through his body, he turned to face Cam. Not trusting himself, Jack secured his hands in his pockets. He knew himself and he wanted, more than anything, to wipe the arrogant smirk from Cam's face. He also knew he couldn't afford the lawsuit that would follow.

"Cam, you're an asshole. I'm sick of you toying with people, intentionally hurting others, just because it gives you a hard-on."

"Not the fucking cape again. Jack, I set you up with a lot of work, and Rebecca isn't bad on the eyes. She could lose a few pounds, but you really should be thanking me."

"Cam, I swear if you fucking ever…I'll…"

"You'll what?" Cam said.

"Fuck it, and fuck you!"

"I think you're the one who with the hard-on. Rebecca, perhaps? Is that it?"

"Fuck you, Cam."

"I never knew you liked your women a little on the, well, chubby side?"

"You're nothing but a piece of shit, Cam." Jack shook his head in disgust, grabbed his coffee off the cab of his truck, and drove away.

Driving away, Jack thought of Cam's words. Sure, Rebecca was easy on the eyes, a rare beauty with a beautiful smile, a bonus for sure. But restoring the cape had a deeper meaning for him. It was part of Eden's history. It was special. His own family's history in

Eden went back generations. That first day, the look in Rebecca's eyes when she spoke about the house, well, that touched him and spoke volumes about what the house meant to her. Like the house and the land, if he was honest with himself, she pulled at him.

Chapter 10

With one hand on the steering wheel and the other playing with Rebecca's extra house key, Cam contemplated his next step. The encounter with Jack at the Coffee Corner was hard to shake off. Cam's shame felt toxic as it surged through his body like a hot poker. *Why did I let Jack Corcoran get the better of me? Jack will always be Eden's shining boy scout and that is part of the rub. I can never hold a candle to Jack.*

Cam held no misconceptions—he knew his family was white trash. He'd grown up hearing the hushed whispers and seen plenty of not so subtle looks when he walked by. Community gossiping about his family's dysfunction was a favorite pastime in this small town. His father's alcoholism and violence, the run-ins with the law, and Cam's trips in and out of State's custody. Yup, while he was growing up, his family was a mess and good entertainment for a sleepy rural town. Hell, he'd even overheard someone yesterday, at the Coffee Corner, describe him as, "Slick with a touch of slime." Cam knew the fine citizens of Eden boxed him in years ago, and there was no turning back or changing their perception. *Why the fuck do I care?*

Slick with a touch of slime, well okay, I can live with that, he thought, *I am no fucking boy scout.* "Why don't we let Rebecca choose for herself?" Cam said as he rubbed the key between his fingers some more,

51

imagining how he'd used those fingers on Rebecca to make her come. *Now Jack can have my sloppy seconds instead of the other way around. Oh, I could provide some help, some relief, some sexual healing. I know women. And Rebecca is a woman who needs a good lay.*

With that thought, he eased the luxury coupe on to Preston Road. Spying her vehicle, his excitement mounted. He paused as he opened the car door and listened for her dogs. No barking—*where the hell are they?* He was disappointed she would miss the opening act, his strut from the car to the house. He loved the build-up, relished giving a lady a preview of the coming attraction.

He knocked on the front door, waited, and knocked again. *Shit, where the hell was she?* He was going to use the key as an excuse to see her. Claim that, whoops, he forgot to give it to her at the closing, but now a sudden change in plans. He'd surprise her, let himself in with the key, and set the scene.

****

After spending the good part of the morning reconfiguring her website and sending out marketing material for her editing services, Rebecca decided to spend a peaceful hour in the woods picking blackberries. As she headed back to the house with her dogs in tow, she thought of the dessert she'd make with the fresh berries. Upon reaching the clearing, a cloud of mist condensed and surrounded her, making it difficult to see her dogs in the thick of it. She stood silently in the mist and called out for Max and Manny to stay. The dip in air temperature had goosebumps forming up and down her arms.

It was then that the mist cleared and she saw the outline of two figures by the pond—a silhouette of a woman clutching a small child. Their bodies rocking together, back and forth. At the sound of footsteps, she glanced back half expecting to find someone or something behind her. When she turned back to the woman and child, the image had disappeared. Her dogs sat at her heels and whimpered. For a moment, she stared at the pond, waiting for them to reappear. A heaviness settled in her chest, not quite comprehending what the pair wanted from her.

Over the years, Rebecca's comfort level with the spirit world had increased. It had taken time. Initially, it put her on edge, but the more she'd denied a spirit's existence the craftier the spirit became in getting her attention. If she gained anything from experience, spirits were persistent. She was empathetic when she realized she was only a conduit for the spirit world to communicate with loved ones.

As she opened the back door to the kitchen, the dogs eyed the squirrel prancing about in the front yard and raced in pursuit. She placed the berries on the big kitchen table, moved to the stove to put on the tea kettle, and set the temperature in the oven for the crisp. She took out two big bowls, placed the bowls on the counter, and started to sift through her cupboards for ingredients.

She reached up to massage her temples. The echoes of a headache forming behind her eyes had her taking a minute. *A hot shower would do the trick,* she thought to herself, *once the crisp is in the oven.* She decided after the shower to hunker down with her contact list and send out more inquiries for work. She also needed to call her parents. Use them as a sounding board to review her plan to earn extra money to cover the house repairs. She valued her parents' sage advice, knew Ellie and Tom McCabe were the voice of reason and would steer her in the right direction.

As she worked on mixing the ingredients for the crisp, the pounding in her head intensified. Hearing Lulu hissing in the other room, Rebecca went to investigate. The sound of a scream reverberated in her head, and she realized it was coming from her. Instinctually, her hand rushed to her chest to calm her heart. She stared in disbelief at Camden Winters, who sat quietly on her living room couch, legs crossed, with a smile that made her skin crawl.

"Sorry, I didn't mean to frighten you, Rebecca. Boy, the look on your face was priceless. I don't think your cat likes me."

The sound of snickering had her stomach lurching. "What the hell are you doing here? How'd you get in?" She noticed it then, a dark aura, the color of red with tints of black specks. His mouth contorted with a grin that had her legs shaking with fear. *Run.* She heard his voice whisper. "What did you say to me?"

"I said I knocked but nobody answered so I thought I would let myself in." He held up the key. "I stopped over to deliver your extra key and…"

He rose and moved toward her.

She held up her hands. "Stop! Put the key on the table in front of you and get out of my house."

"What? I just thought…"

"Cam, if you ever come into my home without my permission again, I'll call the police." She stepped back, inching slowly toward the back door. Her heart hammering in her chest as she calculated her next step.

"I came to deliver your key, you ungrateful bitch," he shot back. He moved closer toward her.

She jabbed her palms against his chest, watched as he lost his footing, and ran for her dogs. She pulled open the back door and with her command, Manny and Max rushed Cam with a low growl.

She heard the swearing from the front room and found him pinned to the front door. Her dogs, teeth bared with deep guttural growls, guarded his every step. Her dog, Max, squared off, nudging Cam's thigh with his head, waiting to be challenged and ready for a fight.

"Call your fucking dogs off or else."

"Not a chance," she said, holding her ground. "You get off my property, or I give my dogs the command to tear you to pieces."

He glared at her and reached behind him to open the front door. It was not until she heard his car peel out that she took a moment to exhale. She gave her dogs the command to relax and allowed herself to sit and cry. She was riled. *Who the hell does he think he is?* She wanted to call her mom, to hear her mom's voice and cry. Lulu wove between her legs, giving her the comfort that she needed.

First things first. She needed to steady her nerves. The last thing she wanted was her mother showing up on her doorstep. An image flashed briefly, one of her at seven, being pulled, hurting, an earlier time she didn't listen to her gut. Rebecca gripped her hands to calm the shaking. *No, not this time. I handled it. Never again will I let a man hurt me.*

Chapter 11

Rebecca woke to the sun on her face, having fallen asleep with her head nestled next to her computer and Lulu cradled in her lap. She found her pups curled up at her feet. By the look of the light, Rebecca figured it was five or six in the morning. She'd spent a good portion of the night checking and rechecking each window and each lock. A night on edge, pacing the floors until exhaustion took hold and she fell asleep.

Rebecca replayed the nightmarish visit from Cam in her head and chastised herself for feeling scared. She knew she had the wits to keep herself safe and felt silly that she'd panicked. Letting herself think she was safe only because she'd moved to a small town was foolish. In her heart and in her experience, she knew there was no such thing as safety. Today she'd make a plan to work out the leftover restlessness and anger that vibrated inside her. Pulling weeds, her mother always said, did the trick.

For Rebecca, concentrating on yard work helped her work through her anger. She threw herself entirely into it and yanked the bull thistle from her flower bed. The physical work helped clear the agitation from her body, although the anger and frustration remained high in her head. What the hell was he thinking? The arrogance! But even more than that, she was pissed that he'd made her feel unsafe in her new home. And, worse yet, the exchange between them brought up past times she'd felt unsafe.

The nerve of it all! She picked up the pulled weeds, dumped them into the wheelbarrow, and set off across the lawn. She glanced at the cape's front steps leaning to the left. Shit. On top of all the nonsense with Cam, she still needed to figure out how she was going to pay for all the repairs. She thought of her personal possessions she could sell. Maybe some of her grandma's jewelry or the painting handed down to her from her grandfather's estate, perhaps even the watch from her parents given to her after she'd graduated from the University of Vermont.

The sound of Jack's truck pulling into her driveway snapped her back to reality. Shading her eyes from the sun, she saw the silhouette of Jack's tall frame approaching her.

"Hey, I'm sorry to come out unannounced," he called out. "I emailed you this morning but thought I would swing by to talk over the proposal I sent. Did you get a chance to read it over?"

"Proposal? Sorry, I didn't even open my email this morning. I had a nasty encounter with Cam Winters yesterday and am still working to shake it off with yard work."

"What the hell happened with Cam?"

His tone and swift reaction indicated there was history there. She learned years ago that she could be her own knight in shining armor. She wouldn't need a man to fight her battles. She was more than capable. Plus, she had two big dogs and her wits. "Nothing I can't handle, or better yet, nothing two big German shepherds and I can't handle. I'm fine. Actually, I'm trying my best not to dwell on it. Can we change the subject?"

"Of course, if that's what you want. How about we read the proposal together?"

"I would love to take a look."

He handed her his copy. She started to read, confused, and then met his eyes.

"You want to barter for the repairs?"

"Well, Corcoran and Sons needs help with marketing. I know you did some work for the Burlington Review. I read the write-up in Vermont Life. I clicked on the website you designed, which by the way was slick. The company credits you for helping them enhance their reputation and increase their client base. I just thought this way we could help each other."

"Jack, this is very generous, but this is a bit out of my skill set. Are you sure?"

"See here," he said, pointing at a line item in the proposal, "this is just a conservative guess of hours, but in all honesty, I think this could work."

Rebecca felt his body brush up against hers, felt the heat of his skin and the clean smell of soap.

"Again, this is a rough estimate for the repairs. We can proceed at a pace that feels comfortable for you." He inched closer, their arms brushing up against each other. Her heart all but stopped. "I think we should start with the landscape, at least cut the high grass around the house and get some wood in before the temperature drops. My father, Henry, added this bit here about website development. He wants a cleaner more up-to-date website for Corcoran and Sons that, in his words, has a bit of flash."

"Flash?" Rebecca said with a slight grin. "Well,

it's always good to stay on the cutting edge."

"Believe me, we have a lot of ideas to bounce off you."

"Wonderful. Developing intimacy, knowing how your company breathes is the only way to truly capture its heart and essence online."

"I know your specialty is in editing text and marketing, but seeing what you did for the Burlington company, I think you can handle our little company just fine."

"Jack, this is exciting and very generous." Rebecca grinned and met his eyes. "Come in. I've got some coffee brewing."

Stepping into the mudroom off the kitchen, she wiped her muddy boots on the mat and went to the cupboard for cups. Coming to the table with two big mugs of coffee, she picked up the proposal again.

"So, are you up for the challenge?" His eyes searched hers. "It's a win-win for both of us," he said.

Rebecca met his gaze. "Okay, then, where do I sign?"

Jack reached into his back pocket and handed her the pen. Their hands met briefly, and she let her fingers lace with his momentarily. With a deep breath, she savored the feeling of his hand for a moment more and signed the contract.

"Do I smell pie?" he asked, sniffing the air.

"Crisp and, yes, you do."

"I thought I smelled something delicious."

"You, Jack Corcoran, are worse than my dogs. Dogs and men, I swear are both ruled by food!"

"I can't say I've ever had a woman compare me to a dog, well, until now. How about we celebrate the signing of the contract with crisp?"

"I think that could be arranged."

"Does that mean I get crisp?"

"Yes, of course, I'll get you some crisp." She moved to the counter, retrieved plates from the cupboard, took her time to steady her excitement. She wondered if he had any idea how hot he was or his effect on her.

"I'm like my father. I have a weakness for sweets, especially pie and crisp. Is it apple or berry?"

"Berry. It's too early for apple." She moved to refill the mugs from the coffeepot. "Would you like vanilla ice cream on the side?"

"Of course!"

She spooned out a generous scoop of vanilla ice cream next to the warm crisp and handed the plate to Jack.

His eyes twinkled as he ate, and it tickled her.

"This is amazing. Best crisp ever!"

She watched a trickle of berry juice escape his lips. With her eyes, she followed its trail as it cascaded down his lip slowly making its way to his chin. She was mesmerized by the red trickle, staining everything in its path. "You, you have a bit of…of…Oh, what the hell." She grabbed his face, kissed, and licked the warm, sweet juice from his mouth. Devouring the sweetness of the berry's juice from his lips.

Her movements were a bit clumsy at first as she moved onto his lap. The heat and smell of his body completely enveloped her senses. All thought went out the window, and she went with instinct and curved her body even tighter around his. She felt his hands on her and his lips on her mouth.

The heat from his kiss was immediate—her body trembled from its impact, her hands moved up his back to hold and to steady the quake. With her hands she outlined every muscle chiseled, inch by inch, in the hard planes of him under her eager fingertips.

She shivered as he traced his hands down the curve of her breasts. He caressed, softly kneading, pulling a moan from low in her throat. Her hands tugged at his shirt when all of a sudden Max and Manny erupted into a frenzy—a knock at the door.

"What the hell?" he whispered in her ear, his hands holding her to him.

"Shit," she said and wiggled free, off his lap to sit on the edge of the chair next to him. "I forgot about the plumber, the one you recommended. She's here." Straightening, Rebecca smoothed out her shirt and pulled the loose strands of her hair back into a hair tie. "How do I look?"

"Umm," he hesitated.

"What is it, Jack?"

"I can't believe it. A plumber that's on time! What are the odds?"

With a laugh, she headed to the door and called back, "Stay for dinner tonight."

"I'd love to."

****

He saw them as clear as day through the binoculars. Watched as the woman pestered and lured the man into her lair. She was worse than a doe in heat. It made him sick. How she used her body to entice, seduce, like a common whore, filling the house with wickedness. Binoculars in hand, he sat in the woods off the back of the house. Sneered as she allowed herself to be fondled, like most whores—a tease, using food to seduce.

How dare she soil his family's home. A house built out of purity, once again being tarnished by a harlot's lust. Spying on her fueled his need to punish, to teach, to force her to obey. To take back what was his birthright. He was trained well—he knew God's plan and knew what needed to be done. He leaned against the tree, spit a couple of times, and rubbed himself. He cursed her wicked power over him. Her lust forcing him to touch himself.

Thoughts of punishing her filled his head. He imagined her on her knees, pleading for mercy. Begging for his forgiveness, all which served to stroke his lust. His release came quickly. He steadied his breath as his seed slowly dripped down the bark of the tree. *A present, something to remember me by, give the little slut something to work for.*

It was then as he started to pull up his pants he heard the child's giggling. He swung around and felt the sudden pop in his groin. The pain dropped him to his knees. In a fetal position, he cupped himself and waited for the pain to subside. He cursed his weakness, his lust, and prayed for God's forgiveness. He knew the pain in his groin was God's punishment for his lustful deed. He'd punish himself, use the rubber band again, and through the pain he'd learn to not give in to his temptation. He needed a new plan.

First thing, he needed to secure a new lookout, one not tarnished with his seed. He would bide his time, wait and watch, like his father taught him. A good hunter studied his prey. One part patience, and one part luck. Luck was on his side, blessed be God who brought her to him, and now he would wait to strike.

Chapter 12

As Jack towed his orange tractor to Rebecca's place, he thought of the night before. Her invitation to stay for dinner, sharing a meal, talking for hours, and the goodnight kiss that lingered a bit too long. He'd only come by yesterday to talk over the proposal; the rest was a welcome surprise. *Pretty damn perfect,* he thought. As he drove, he calculated the time it would take to haul out the downed trees. He knew he had to get the landscape cleaned up before he could tackle cutting the grass. Rebecca agreed that getting wood in was a priority, so he'd start there. Jack's mind wandered back to the kiss last night, making it all but impossible to focus on work. He couldn't get her off his mind.

He surveyed the land, located some fallen trees he could cut up. After, he'd set out to take down more trees to get the three cords of wood she'd need to heat this old cape through the winter. Jack loved working outside, he preferred it, breathing in the air, working with his hands, hauling wood, seeing the unexpected wildlife passing through. It didn't get any better.

As he started up the old orange tractor, it sputtered and coughed a bellow of dark smoke. "Shit," he said as he jumped off and threw open the cab. Keeper, his Irish Wolfhound, moved to stand along next to him.

Jack turned and caught her gaze. The eye contact

pierced his chest. She was a mystery, the kiss the other day so unexpected but so full of heart-stopping heat. A hot punch that hit him in the heart, the gut, and his...*Jesus, he was falling hard and quick.*

She waved and gave him a wide grin.

He returned the smile and felt his face heat up. *Jesus, man, get a grip.* Truth was he couldn't get her off his mind. She stirred him up in a good way, but it had him feeling ungrounded. He was not only "walking on air" but walking in the fucking clouds.

The dogs found their way to Keeper for a thorough butt sniffing before turning their attention to Jack, who petted their black and tan coats. As the dogs walked off, Jack turned back to the tractor and tried to focus on the task at hand. He truly believed she didn't have any idea how amazing and how utterly distracting she was.

"Trouble?" she asked.

"Nope, just needed more oil." He turned toward the tractor, oil can in hand, and started to pour.

"Can you show me?" She leaned closer in, watching as he poured the oil.

"Right here," he said, pointing.

Rebecca leaned in a bit closer yet, slightly brushing her body against his. The faint scent of rose on her body was intoxicating. He suddenly had the impulse to embrace her, felt himself go hard, and turned away. *Damn near impossible to get work done with her body so close.* What he wanted to do was take her on the lawn. He didn't care who saw them. He needed to feel himself in her, her strong legs around him, every muscle inside her exploring every inch of him. Not saying a word, he stood abruptly and walked back to his truck.

"Well, I'll leave you to it," she said, turning toward the house.

****

Leave you to it? I'm losing my mind over this guy. What I really want is to jump your bones. Rebecca called to her dogs and headed in, breathing to steady her racing heart. Maybe a cold shower instead, cold water would clear her head and cool off the fire burning in her body.

Instead of the shower, Rebecca busied herself examining the material Jack put together on his company's history. She opened up her laptop to organize the information on the company's target audience, goals, and objectives for the company's website. She added some basic layout concepts to her idea board and calculated she had a couple of hours to work on the website before her conference call.

As she started to type, a jolt of electricity had her hands tingling. She checked out the connections on the laptop. *Odd,* she thought, *old house could mean old wiring.* Her eyes flicked back to the screen, and then she felt the rush. The familiar panic in her head and in her gut. Rebecca rose from her desk and saw Lulu lazing in the kitchen window.

"Well, you're okay." She stopped to give the cat's belly a quick rub. "Okay, now let's go check on the boys." She walked outside to the front lawn where she'd left the dogs lying in the grass. As soon as she stepped around the corner of the house, she heard him. Heard the swearing and found him lying on the ground by the tractor.

"Fuck! Fuck! Fuck me! Fucking tree!" Jack, flat on his back, held his leg high, a branch protruding from his right thigh.

She ran and knelt down in the grass beside him. "Leave it! Leave it alone. Don't move!" she commanded. "If you keep moving it will bleed more."

"Easy for you to say. It *fucking* hurts!"

She inspected the damage and sprang into action. "Where's your phone?"

"Back pocket. What are you doing?"

Before she could answer, she had the phone out of his pocket and dialed 911. "This is Rebecca McCabe, old Parker place on Preston Road. I have Jack Corcoran on the ground with an injury to his right thigh. A branch is lodged in the thigh. There's heavy bleeding seeping out of the wound. He needs an ambulance right away. Please hurry!" She hung up and grabbed his hand.

He rolled his eyes. "Great, now the whole fucking town will know. Did you have to call 911?"

"You're turning paler by the minute. You're bleeding all over my grass. So yes, I had to call 911. Suck it up, Jack. You need a hospital."

"I'll be fine, just help me pull it out," he said, his face tensing as he shifted his body.

"Stop moving," she ordered. She put her hand on him to keep him still.

"I want it out!" he roared.

"Stay still! Do you trust me?" she asked, her green eyes fixed on his.

"Yes, I do, I do trust you."

"Then stay still and do what I say."

"Jesus, Mary, mother of god, it fucking hurts."

"Jack, they're almost here. I see the lights." She turned just in time to see the ambulance pull in. She watched the big bald man, an easy 275 pounds of pure muscle, as he exited the passenger side of the ambulance. He was followed by a woman, who also was seriously jacked, exiting out of the driver's side.

"Jesus, brother, you've done good this time,"

"Dewey, just pull it out!"

"Grady, get the gurney, we are going to need to take my bonehead brother in," Dewey called out.

"Brother?" Rebecca asked.

The burly man turned and offered her his hand. "Dewey Corcoran. I'm Jack's big brother," he said, working to secure Jack's leg.

"Big is an understatement. Dewy, can you please pull it out?" Jack asked, his voice weak.

"Brother, if I pull this out, you might bleed out. The branch might have nicked an artery. Stay still," Dewey ordered.

"You the owner?" Dewey motioned with his head to the house.

"Yes, Rebecca McCabe."

Grady aligned the gurney, as Dewey readied his brother's body.

"Okay, Grady, on three. 1-2-3." As they lifted Jack's body a soft moan escaped from his lips.

"Jesus, Dewey."

"Sorry, brother, we'll get you there soon."

Rebecca caught Jack's grimace and quickly grabbed his hand. "You're going to be okay. I will be right behind you. I'm coming to the hospital."

"Keeper!" Jack eyeballed Rebecca and then his brother Dewey.

"Keeper can stay here. He'll be fine, don't worry," she said.

Dewey turned to Rebecca. "This hardhead is going

to be fine. It's going to take more than a little branch to bring him down. Grady, let's go. It will be faster to take Center Road to the hospital."

As soon as Dewey closed the doors of the ambulance Rebecca felt the ache in her heart and the tears flowed.

Chapter 13

To Rebecca, it seemed like forever to get to the hospital, but in reality, it was only twenty minutes away. She followed closely behind the ambulance, wiping tears from her eyes as she drove.

As Dewey and Grady wheeled Jack into the ER, Rebecca followed close behind. She saw a small clan gathered around him, suspecting this was Jack's family. Rebecca hung back and waited.

"What the hell happened?" said the ER nurse with flaming red hair, who stood at command at Jack's side.

"Freak accident, tree branch lodged into Jack's right thigh."

A nurse inspected the wound. "Jesus, this doesn't look good. How much blood loss?" she said, as she checked his breathing.

"Significant," Dewey said as he wiped at the sweat from his forehead. His partner Grady handed him a bottle of water. "Thanks, Grady."

"I'm okay, Mom, Dad, Maureen, I'm fine."

"Maureen, please take care of your baby brother," the older woman said.

Rebecca noticed how the woman's hands rubbed at the beads of a rosary.

"No worries, Mama. He's going to be fine," she said, wheeling Jack behind the curtain.

Dewey turned to the ER registration and motioned

his parents. "Mom, Dad can you check Jack in?"

"Yes. Of course." The old couple moved to sit down with the clerk at the desk, the man holding the woman's hand.

Rebecca found Dewey, sitting in the corner, drinking water with his partner Grady.

"Dewey! Is he going to be all right?"

"Rebecca, he's going to be just fine." Dewey motioned to Grady. "Grady, would you mind taking Rebecca to the cafeteria for some water and get a detailed account of what happened today?"

"Of course." Grady led Rebecca down the hall.

Maureen Corcoran observed her brother and Grady as they talked with the brunette. As Grady led her away, Maureen approached her brother. "Who's the chick?"

"A friend of Jack's," Dewey put two hands up in surrender, "that's all I know. I just met her. She bought the old Parker place. Jack was out there, working."

"Is that so? Was he hurt on the job?"

"Looks that way. Grady is talking with her now to find out how it happened."

"Good, I'll be right back. I'm not done talking to you, so don't you dare leave," she ordered.

"You know where to find me, Maureen." Dewey crossed the room and took a seat next to Rebecca who sat, with Grady, drinking a cup of coffee. "How's the coffee?" he asked Rebecca.

"Horrible. I should've listened to you and picked up water. How is he?"

"He's going to be okay, Rebecca."

"I just wished I'd found him quicker." Rebecca stared at the curtain.

"Jack's a strong man. He takes after his father and

71

his big brother of course. Why don't you come over and meet my parents?" Dewey said, offering her his hand.

Millie and Henry Corcoran sat huddled together, providing comfort for the other.

"Mom, Dad, this is Rebecca. Sorry, Rebecca, I didn't catch your last name."

"McCabe. Your son was working out at my place when the accident happened. I'm so sorry," she said, feeling a pang of guilt in the pit of her stomach.

"Not your fault. Comes with the work. My boy is tough as nails. There is always a danger of getting hurt when you work with your hands. I'm Henry, and this is my wife, Millie," he said, patting her hand.

"Yes, dear. You should know. It's nice to meet you, Rebecca, come and sit," Millie said.

"You're the gal who's building my company's website," Henry said as he nodded to Rebecca and removed his glasses. "Honey, she bought the Parkers' old place."

Rebecca noted the subtle tenderness between them and had a brief moment picturing her parents.

"I love the pond out back of your house. It's a beautiful pond, full of wildlife. I love the path too, and how the pond is set so privately in the woods, yet sometimes I get a feeling of…" Millie stopped.

"What? A feeling of what?"

"Well, it's hard to explain, dear, almost a feeling of 'missingness' at that pond, like I said, it's hard to explain." Millie shot her an amused smile and shook her head. "I'm just rambling on like an old woman. I'm glad you love that old place. A place like that, not just the house but the land, needs an owner who feels deeply connected to it." Millie winked as she gave

Rebecca's hand a quick squeeze.

Storming through the ER doors with her red hair tied back in a no-nonsense ponytail, Maureen Corcoran entered the waiting room. Her lips pressed tightly together as she scanned her notes. She headed straight for her parents but stopped abruptly, her blue eyes zeroing in on Rebecca who sat talking to her mother. "So, it looks like Jack is going to need to be admitted for at least a couple of days. It's not bad, but he did need a blood transfusion and some fluids. Doc Adams sutured the wound. Jack might need a skin graft, but Doc wants to wait it out. Wants to wait and see how it heals before making that decision. Jack received a lot of stitches, and he's on a strong course of antibiotics. The branch missed an artery by millimeters, thank God, but he still lost a lot of blood. He's going to be weak, sore, and bruised, but he's damn lucky."

"Thank God," Millie echoed as she laid her head on Henry's shoulder and kissed her rosary to her lips.

Rebecca patted Millie's knee reassuringly.

"I don't think we met. I'm Maureen Corcoran, Jack's older sister."

Rebecca felt the cold, frosty blue stare, a stare that could rip holes through concrete. "I'm Rebecca McCabe. Your brother was working out at my place when the accident happened."

"You did some quick thinking, Rebecca. It could've been a lot worse if you didn't find him. I know my baby brother, and he can be a bit of a hardhead. Wouldn't put it past him to keep working with a branch protruding from his leg."

"Sounds like my boy," Henry said proudly.

"Sounds like his idiot father and why my hair is

gray. Can we see him, Maureen?" Millie asked.

"You know the rules, only family," Maureen said, meeting Rebecca's eyes.

As the family walked off, Dewey stopped. "Hey, I'll let him know you were here, and don't worry, Doc Adams is old but the best. He delivered every one of us. Jack's in good hands. How about I call you with an update?"

"That would be great. Thank you, Dewey."

"No problem. You want me to come and pick up Keeper later?"

"No, no, Keeper's fine. He'll love the playdate with my dogs, believe me."

"Okay, then," He turned to leave, paused, and glanced back. "You know, you could visit tomorrow, during visiting hours if you want, and again, thanks for everything you did for Jack today."

As Dewey walked away, Rebecca slumped down into the chair and wiped at the tears in her eyes.

Chapter 14

Rebecca woke up in bed the next morning feeling exhausted, having spent the night tossing and turning with more unpleasant dreams and a radiating pain in her right leg. The connection to Jack was, most likely, the cause of the pain in her leg. If history had taught her anything, she knew the signs of reading someone—feeling their physical and emotional pain was part of it. In the middle of the night, she'd been woken by the sound of a child giggling. She wondered about children who lived and, maybe, died in her house in the past, and thought, perhaps, she was dealing with a spirit.

Her dream last night nagged at her, like the image at the pond, a little girl skipping on the path, a man holding her hand, dressed in all black. The man scowled, pulling at the little girl's arm, rushing her. Again, Cam stood next to Rebecca in the dream. This time though there was a woman in the dream. A woman who was frantic, searching—moving from room to room in the house. As she searched, the woman called out a name. *What was it? Silas, no not Silas. Selene, maybe?* Frustrated, Rebecca gave up trying to force it. *What were the dreams telling her? Why this little girl? Why Cam? What did they want from her?*

Rebecca stretched and made a mental list for the day. She had to get some design work started, especially a rough draft of the Corcoran and Sons website. She loved a good challenge and already had some ideas brewing. But first, she needed to visit Jack in the hospital. It hurt knowing how much pain he was in, and she harbored some guilt that he'd been injured working for her.

As she straightened the bed's comforter sporting a pattern of spring purple crocuses eager to bloom, she mulled over her own willingness to open up. *Am I ready to finally bloom, willing to take charge?* Her connection to Jack was strong. Deep down she was a romantic, and she sensed Jack was looking for more than a sexual relationship. It was more than just sex for her, and she hoped she was reading him correctly.

"Okay guys, who needs to go potty?" And with those words, her two German shepherds sprang up. She found Keeper at the foot of the stairs. Noticing the blanket on the couch that she laid out was a mess, she knew he'd found his spot. "Good boy! How'd you sleep?" She bent to give Keeper a good scratch behind the ears, and after all the dogs did a thorough sniffing of each other, opened the door.

She went to the kitchen, switched on the coffee maker, and checked her phone—a text from Jack.

—*R, thx again for everything. I owe u. How's my boy Keep doing? J.*—

Her heart did a little dance, the tension melted from her shoulders, and she responded.

—*J, Keeper is doing great. He's enjoying his playdate. Dewey mentioned I could swing by today if that's okay? I'd love to see you. R.*—

—*R. What time can you get here???? Kissy emoji J.*—

This time she jumped for joy.

She decided to dress, feed the dogs, grab her "to go" cup, and head over to the hospital. She needed to see Jack in person—seeing him would provide all the relief she was seeking. Sensing her excitement, her cat Lulu jumped on the counter to nudge her hand. Rebecca stroked Lulu's back, and the cat arched up against her hand. "Little one, I just need to put eyes on him, all of him. Coffee, Jack, library, then work. Right, Lulu?" And Lulu purred in agreement.

Chapter 15

A quick coffee, that's all Cam wanted when he pulled into the Eden General Store. As he parked his car, he noticed the meeting of the super-duty pickups out front, or what Cam liked to call the SDGC, better known as "the Super-Duty Gossip Club." He overheard the murmurings amongst the gathering, all redneck friends of Jack, concerned about his accident. All he wanted was a God damn coffee, so he'd grab it quickly before they tried to rope him into talking. Moving to the counter, he noticed the big glass collection jar and read the sign, "Donations welcomed for Jack Corcoran's hospital bills. Speedy recovery, friend! We love you, Jack! Any amount welcomed."

"Phht, you gotta be kidding me," he said pointing to the jar. The clerk behind the counter only shrugged.

"Hey, Cam, did you hear about Jack? Do you want to donate to his recovery?"

Cam turned to find Jack's work puppy, better known as Jeb Hatch, behind him in line, holding a box of donuts and a get well card.

"No, thanks, but my sportscar needs a new paint job, donations welcomed." He picked up his coffee, gave Jeb an exaggerated eye roll, and turned on his heels toward the door.

"Nice fucking attitude, Cam!"

"Save it for someone who cares," he said without a

backward glance.

Sitting in his car, Cam watched the lot of them, talking about, praying about Jack Corcoran. Everywhere he went, all he heard was Jack's name. Jack's accident, poor Jack's leg, will Jack live to work again, there was no end to the stories.

"Fucking town," he muttered. He was sick to death of hearing about Jack Corcoran. *I need to leave this town.* For decades, he'd dealt with the town's judgment of him. He'd grown tired of smalltown ways. *Who the fuck made them judge and jury?*

Cam thought about his visit to Rebecca's place. It hadn't turned out the way he had planned. He'd miscalculated. He'd expected Rebecca to get wet and drop her pants just from seeing him sitting on her couch. She should be grateful he found her even remotely attractive, the extra weight and all. The ungrateful bitch and those damn dogs of hers—actually threatened him with bodily harm and the State Police! Who the hell did she think she was? *No one threatens Camden Winters, especially a fucking outsider.* He would teach her a lesson.

Truthfully, he felt the blow of it, her dismissal, her rejection of him, and the shame slithered like a snake in his belly. He needed a plan, maybe it was time for history to repeat itself. Rebecca didn't know his family's history, the rumors about his parents, and Cam's stints in State's custody. He'd turn up the Cam charm to get back into her good graces, make amends, and earn her trust again. Flowers, he'd bring her the most obnoxious bouquet of flowers he could find, and wine, yes, white wine. He'd put on a show. Practice the flowery apology, hope we can be friends…the whole nine yards, and then fuck with her.

Chapter 16

"How you doing, baby brother?" Jack's older identical twin sisters, Maureen and Kathleen, said in unison as they entered his room, carrying what looked to be a small army of provisions.

"What's all this for? I'm hoping to get out of here today," he said. Jack shook his head—instead of having one mother he had three. Sometimes this made him smile, and other times it made him cringe.

"Let me check the bandage," Maureen said as she inspected the wound.

"I'm fine, stop, I'm fine. I want out of here!"

Maureen and Kathleen shook their heads no in unison.

"Jack, you need to listen to the doctors. Be good," Kathleen said, arranging and tidying the room.

God, he hated when his sisters made him feel like he was still five to their ten years. Jack watched as Kathleen struggled to bend over to pick up a magazine on the floor.

"Leave it, Kathleen. Jesus, you're eight months pregnant, and if you go into labor, I will never hear the end of it from that husband of yours. The last thing I need is Greg blaming me for you overdoing it. Where is he anyway?"

"The kids want to visit you, so he is bringing Mimi and Aiden later today. Mimi is taking it hard. She

81

doesn't like to see her favorite uncle hurt."

Hearing this made Jack's chest feel heavy. "God, I love those kids."

"I know. They're the best. And you're a great uncle, Uncle Fun, they love you. So if you can avoid getting hurt, that would help."

"I'll see what I can do," he said, as he shifted in the bed.

"You okay?"

"Yeah, just hurts like a son-of-a-bitch. I feel bad about Mimi."

"She cried herself to sleep worried about you last night. It will help her to come visit. She needs to see for herself that her uncle is alive and well. Her imagination doesn't quit."

"I'll make sure she knows Uncle Fun is fine."

"You do that, brother. I love you," Kathleen said, hand on her belly, shifting her weight to one leg to bend down, and gave him a quick kiss on the forehead.

"I'm off. I need to meet with Dr. Erickson for what I hope is the last time, right buddy?" Kathleen rubbed her enormous belly.

"Good luck, Kathleen."

Jack watched as Kathleen stopped to whisper to her twin. Both giggled, the same exact giggle, and laughed some more. Jack knew this secret language of his twin sisters meant they were up to something.

"What the hell was all that about?" he asked, catching the smirk Maureen shared with her twin before the door closed.

"None of your business, baby brother. Are you comfortable? How's the pain 0-10?" Maureen studied Jack with nurse's eyes.

"I have a nurse. Be a good sister and fetch me a hamburger."

"Nice try, not a chance. I will check on you later. Try to rest. I love you."

"Love you too, Maureen."

Chapter 17

With his sisters finally gone, Jack laid his head back against the pillow and let his mind wander to that first day he'd watched Rebecca in the field—her laugh, her body, the green eyes. *God, how I would love to take her in that field someday.* He imagined the softness of her body, her taste, his heart with hers. His hands peeling off her jeans, laying her down on a blanket in the middle of that field. The soft lace he imagined she wore underneath. His fingers slipping under the lace— exploring, touching, savoring her depths. Her need, crying out for more as he touched her.

His phone vibrating on the side table shook him out of his fantasy. He ran a hand down his erection, feeling the ache in his body as well as his heart. One thing he was sure about: he wanted more than just sexual relief. His hookups with Melanie were good but just took care of a need, and they both had known they were using each other. Friends with benefits and if memory served, it was good for both of them, at least for the short term. *I want more, and I want more with Rebecca.*

"Hey, man. You're a sight for sore eyes." Jeb Hatch stood in the doorway, the only non-relative who worked for Corcoran and Sons.

"Hey Jeb, you didn't need to stop by."

"I wanted to check out if I was moving up in the family business." Jeb snickered and gave Jack a man hug.

"Very funny, asshole. You're fucking hilarious."

"I brought you donuts and a card."

"Donuts! I think I love you. Hand them over."

"Don't you want to read the card first?"

"No. By the way, how's the studying going?" he asked, taking a big bite out of the chocolate donut.

The question had Jeb pacing the length of the hospital room. "It's totally stressing me out, but I'm determined to pass. Ninety questions are completely excessive in my opinion. I totally suck at multiple choice, but soon Corcoran and Sons will have an electrician on board."

"Yep, we will. You got this. Stop stressing."

****

Maureen Corcoran entered Jack's hospital room, looking down at the paperwork in her hands. "I think I dropped my…" Seeing Jeb, she stopped, felt her breath catch in her chest.

She noticed how his eyes traveled down her body. *God, why does he keep staring at me? I must look like shit.* Turning around, she quickly moved a stray piece of hair behind her ear before moving to Jack's side.

"Jack, I didn't know you had company. Sorry, I'll get out of your way," she said, trying to make a hasty retreat.

"Maureen, stay, it's just Jeb."

"Hey, Jeb, long time no see." She tried not to stare as she took in his rugged face. She knew he was way too young for her, but God, was he pretty to look at. *The gods and goddesses, hell the whole universe, took their time sculpting this one.* His smoky gray eyes and a body jacked with precision. *Jesus, what I wouldn't give for fifteen minutes alone with him. On second thought, make that a solid hour.*

"Hey, Maureen, you taking good care of your brother?"

Lost in Jeb's smoky eyes she didn't register the question. Snapping to she saw their confused faces staring back at her.

"I'm sorry, what did you say?"

"I asked if you were taking care of your brother?"

"Jesus, Maureen, get your head out of the clouds." Jack joked.

"As you can see, Jeb, I'm trying to, but he's a major pain in the ass."

"I totally get it. You should see him on a job. If I had a nickel for every—"

"Umm, guys, I'm right here. I'm the patient, the one who's hurt. No talking about me in front of me."

"Like you would let us ever forget," Maureen said as she rolled her eyes at her brother.

Rebecca knocked gently on the door and entered holding a large bouquet of wildflowers.

Jack caught her eye. "I hope you snuck some beer and chili fries in with those flowers," he said, smiling.

"Anyone going to introduce me?" Jeb asked.

"No way! Just kidding, buddy. This is Rebecca McCabe. She hired us out at the old Parker place. Rebecca, this is one of my best friends and partner, Jeb Hatch. You will be seeing him out at your place soon, especially when we tackle your electrical needs."

"Nice to meet you, Jeb. How's our patient?" Rebecca moved to Jack's side.

"I'm good, bored, but good. Going to leave a hell of a scar."

"Scars are sexy," she returned with a wink.

"I'm glad you think so," he said, brushing his fingertips lightly over her hand.

"Rebecca, if you like scars, let me show you some," Jeb said, playfully lifting his shirt to reveal a scar on his chest. He shot Maureen a bashful grin. Maureen played along, moved to lift her shirt up.

"Yeah, I've got a huge scar from my appendix being taken out when I was eight. It's a real beauty."

"Okay, you two, very funny. And now if you two don't mind, I have some business to discuss with my new client." Jack said.

"I bet you do." Jeb snickered.

Chapter 18

As Rebecca closed the hospital door behind Maureen and Jeb, she caught the intense aura swirl around their two bodies in a perfect circle. "Well, I'll be."

"What was that?" Jack asked.

"Jeb's a great guy. Does your sister realize he's got a major crush on her?"

"Jeb? No way!"

"Yes, Jeb! You didn't notice the way he was looking at her? His face turned five shades of red just standing next to her. And I would put a bet on it that your sister is equally smitten with him."

"Maureen doesn't get smitten. It goes against her nature as a hardass. I didn't notice a thing, and right now the last thing I want to think about is my sister and Jeb."

"I'm glad you're okay," she said, running her fingertips across his brow.

"I am now. Thanks for coming, and thanks for the flowers."

"You had me so worried."

Rebecca laced her fingers with his. Reaching forward, she placed her lips to his mouth. She took her time exploring the soft contours of his lips. She rested her forehead on his for a brief moment, took a deep breath to steady her beating heart, and kissed him again.

She summoned all the courage she could muster and, staring into his eyes, she unbuttoned her top exposing a silk bra the color of soft cream.

With eyebrows slightly lifted and eyes widening, he grabbed her hand. "Rebecca, you don't need to..." He whispered.

"Please, Jack, let me," she whispered back. She took his hand and squeezed it softly as he closed his eyes. When his eyes re-opened, she met his gaze and relaxed a bit more.

"I just had to make sure this was real, and I wasn't dreaming," he said.

Laughing, she leaned forward placing another kiss to his lips, and raised her eyebrows suggestively.

"I think I've just forgotten all my moves. Smooth, Corcoran," he said with a slight laugh.

"I've got it, Jack."

Staring into his eyes, she let the shirt fall away and shivered slightly as he placed a hand over the soft lace of her bra. An eruption of goosebumps formed as his fingers drifted under the straps. He cupped each of her breasts with his hands, used his thumb to outline each of her nipples within the lace. With his touch, her nipples hardened with each stroke of his thumb as he rolled his fingers slowly and methodically over each.

She offered him a sweet smile before leaning forward granting him full access. His lips slowly traced her nipples through the sheer fabric of her bra. A low hum vibrated deep in her throat as the pleasure built between them. She let her hand linger under the hospital sheets to feel him, found him hard, and with her hand rhythmically set the pace. She heard his breathing quicken as he shifted his body with need, his eyes glazed over with desire as she continued.

Pulling back, she exhaled, took a moment to catch her breath.

"Too much?" he asked.

"No, it's perfect," she said, placing both hands behind her back to unclasp her bra. She followed his eyes as he watched her slowly let each strap fall from her shoulders until the bra completely slipped away. As she made eye contact, she ran her hands down her torso to cup each one of her breasts. The expression on his face had her pulse racing. She released her hair, letting it tumble down to her shoulders, landing just shy of her breasts. Shifting her weight, she guided his mouth once again to her breast. As he nuzzled and nipped, she ran a hand back under the sheets to caress him, felt, as his hands pressed her body closer to his and let the heat build once again. She moaned with each new sensation.

"Man, I think I left my cell pho—" Jeb stopped, no doubt having caught an eyeful from the doorway.

Rebecca hurried to cover herself with her shirt.

"Shit, sorry man, sorry Rebecca," he said as he backed out of the room.

With a sideways glance, Rebecca looked at Jack. "Well, that most certainly wasn't part of my plan." She laughed as she secured her bra.

"I would say that was pretty damn perfect until my bonehead buddy rushed the room. I might just have to fire him," he said, helping her with her shirt. She leaned forward and with her lips tugged at his bottom lip.

"How about a raincheck? And, maybe, if you're lucky, next time I'll wear a nurse's uniform." She wiggled her eyebrows seductively at him as he grabbed his heart, feigning a heart attack.

"You are full of surprises, Rebecca McCabe."
"You have no idea, Jack Corcoran."

Chapter 19

As Rebecca headed to the Eden Library, she chewed on her lower lip, still aroused from the heat generated with Jack, and beamed. She all but bounced down the sidewalk, her body abuzz with confidence. Rebecca let her heart guide her and had to admit in return she felt sexy and hoped that maybe after all these years—her turn had finally come. With a big wide smile, she headed up the long granite steps to the library.

Reaching the top step, she stopped and studied the library's architecture, the detail in the old neoclassical design of the building with its elegant, long columns. She had a fondness for libraries, the quiet, the rules, and most of all, getting lost in a good story. As she entered through the massive double wooden doorway, the musty aroma of old books and lemony furniture polish filled her nostrils.

Wandering across the speckled marble floor, Rebecca followed the soft sound of two people whispering. She paused for a brief moment taking pleasure in both the smell and being surrounded by books. To her, books would always comfort her soul. She spotted the librarians standing behind the massive wooden desk.

"Excuse me, sorry to interrupt. I'm wondering if you could help me?" she asked the man who stood behind the desk.

"I'll do my best. What can I help you with?" the man said with a soft-spoken professional manner. He wore a sweater the same color as his blue eyes paired with tan khakis. The man smiled at Rebecca, and she sensed his gentle soul.

"I'm trying to locate some information on the house I just bought. You might know it, the old Parker place on Preston?"

"I do know it. That house is full of history. A real beauty! Your house is one of the oldest houses from the early 1800s still standing in Eden. What specifically are you looking for?"

"Well, I'm curious who built the house, maybe a chronological list of prior occupants, and I'm also wondering if anyone or specifically any children died in the house."

"That's quite a list; let me think for a moment," he said as he reached behind the desk and handed Rebecca a form. "I'm going to have you fill this out. By the way, I'm Tom Attwell, the head librarian here in Eden, and this is my assistant Carol Mahoney. Carol, can you help Ms…?"

"Sorry, I'm Rebecca, Rebecca McCabe."

"Okay, Ms. McCabe, Carol will help you with the form and the research. She is the goddess of research here," he said, giving Carol's shoulder a quick squeeze as he walked away.

"Great, but please call me Rebecca." Rebecca noted Carol played the part of an assistant librarian to perfection, with her waif figure, blonde hair pulled back in a tight bun, and nondescript brown sweater with a plaid skirt, topped off with a pair of large black glasses.

The glasses were a tad too big for her face and seemed to cover up what looked to be huge blue eyes. Carol's eyes reminded her of a Margaret Keane painting. It was hard not to stare.

"How soon do you need this information, Rebecca?" Carol said, her voice measured and efficient as she studied Rebecca over the top of her glasses.

"I'm in no rush. Really, I'm just curious about the old place."

Carol glanced at the calendar on the computer. "As it so happens, I can start on this right away. Tom is working on wrapping up our latest project, so I'm all yours."

"Great, how do we start?"

"Typically, with a project like this, I like to organize chronologically, research past deeds on the property, and go from there. I think it makes the most sense to acquire a complete historical record of deeds on the property which you can request at the town clerk's office. Then move on to the Vermont Vital Records of the early 19th century for information on births, marriages, and deaths of occupants. We should also consider a visit to the Vermont Historical Society."

"The Vermont Historical Society?" Rebecca asked.

"Oh yes, the VHS holds a wealth of historical information and can be a handy resource for this type of project."

Rebecca saw the giddy expression in Carol's eyes and smiled to herself, knowing she hit the jackpot. Carol was a research nerd.

"Should we split it up?"

"Faster that way. If you could work on obtaining the deeds from the town clerk's office, I will contact the

VHS about resources to help guide the project. I know the librarian quite well, and then we should set a date to go. The VHS is down in Barre."

"Sounds good. How do you feel about going together?"

"Certainly, that way we can review the material as we find it," Carol said, checking her calendar. "I have some time open next Wednesday, say noon?"

"Perfect. I'm wondering, I know this sounds like an odd request, and feel free to say no."

"What is it?" Carol said, her big eyes peering again over the top of her glasses.

"I was wondering if you'd be willing to come out to the house and pick me up? I could make us lunch beforehand."

"I suppose we could…"

The expression on Carol's face had Rebecca feeling she might have overstepped.

"It's just, I'm new to the area and know only a handful of people in Eden. Truthfully, Carol, I'm missing my girlfriends in Burlington terribly. I completely understand if you…"

"Actually, Rebecca, that would be nice. I'll see you about noon then."

"Do you need directions?"

"No, everyone who lives in Eden knows the old Parker place. I actually live on Preston, half a mile from your house on the right. Maybe you've seen the house. The small converted sugar house that sits into the woods, opposite side of the road from your house?"

"Yes, I've seen your house. Super cute. It reminds me of a house that would be in a Brothers Grimm fairy tale."

"I get that reference a lot. I think it was part of the reason I bought the house. Don't we all want to live a fairy tale life?"

"I suppose it depends on the fairy tale," Rebecca said with a slight smile.

"Good point, I never was much of a fan of Grimm's 'Hansel and Gretel'."

"What? You have something against a children's story about child abuse and cannibalism?" Rebecca joked. "It's really nice to meet one of my neighbors, finally."

"I've been meaning to stop over and introduce myself but thought I should wait until you were settled. And now when I come over, I can see what you've done with the place."

"It's a work in progress. I'm wondering though…"

"What is it, Rebecca?"

"Well, I know this might seem odd, but have you ever noticed a little blonde girl about, around five or six years old on Preston Road?"

"I can't say I have. Hmm, let me think. No, I don't know of any families having a child that young who live on Preston. Why do you ask?"

"When I drove up the first day, I saw her. She was standing by the edge of the woods. She looked like she just came from a swim. I just thought it strange she didn't have an adult with her. She had me a bit on edge."

"Hmm, well, it's not uncommon for parents out in the country to allow their children a bit more freedom."

"I suppose that could be it," Rebecca said, still concerned.

"I'll keep an eye out and ask around. I'm sure

someone in the neighborhood knows who she is."

"I appreciate it. It was really nice to meet you, Carol."

"You too, Rebecca, I'll see you Wednesday."

****

Seeing Rebecca leave, Tom rushed to join Carol behind the desk.

"What do you think?" Tom said.

"Nice, and, obviously, pretty, in a 1940s Rita Hayworth way." Carol and Tom both sighed, loving the old films and the old stars. He chimed in. "Or better yet, Hedy Lamarr."

"Yes, totally, Hedy Lamarr—the body and the brains. Good call! When you get home, tell Peter we need to have a movie night soon. Maybe Hedy's film 'Ecstasy.' I can certainly see why Jack is falling for her. She's very sensual and smart, a pretty lethal combination."

"You're right, Jack would be all over that."

"Hard for anybody to resist, regardless of which way you lean," Carol considered.

"I can't wait to get home and tell Peter we met Jack's crush. He has been so tightlipped about it. I know he has information. He and Jack are thick as thieves. I just can't get Peter to spill the goods. He's lucky I'm not the jealous type," Tom mused.

"Good thing you and Peter have been together forever. I just wonder how serious this crush is for Jack? And how serious is it for Rebecca?"

"You're worried she's going to hurt our friend."

"Of course, the last thing we need is another woman breaking his heart. Especially after what Alice did to him. That bitch!"

"I don't think I could watch Jack go through another breakup. There were times Peter and I were concerned he wasn't going to climb out of the hole he was in."

"I know how that feels," she said.

"I know you do, honey. But now look at our Jack. He's finally moving on."

"I'm happy for him. I just worry."

"Carol, maybe you should stop worrying about Jack and follow his lead instead and start testing the waters."

"Dating?" She scoffed.

"Yes, dating! It might be time to air out that house of yours."

"Very funny. Believe me, I'm well aware of the cobwebs and the dust in my house."

"Carol, you have the biggest heart in this town and a ton of love to share. Maybe it's time to start sharing it," he said, walking away.

Carol hunched over the desk and sighed.

Chapter 20

Hot, bothered, and bewitched. Jack's father tried to warn him about Irish girls—they'll steal your heart and soul. Hell, he'd seen it with his own parents—the power his mother had over his father, the poor sap. Jack was beginning to believe his father's superstitions and was having trouble staying still as he sat on the edge of the hospital bed. His whole body felt keyed up after Rebecca's visit yesterday. He couldn't recall a time that he was so worked up sexually over a woman, not even Alice. He replayed the hospital bed scene a million times, bewitched indeed. And, with that thought, he grabbed his phone. He wanted to, no, he needed to connect with her. Nervous, his fingers shook slightly as he typed in the text to her.

R. —*The docs finally gave me the ok to go home. Can I swing by? J.*—

He stared down at his phone, said a silent prayer, and willed a response. He closed his eyes and leaned back on the bed. Hearing the ding of the text, his eyes flew open. *Thank you, God.*

J. —*Great. Yes, come by, can't wait to c u. R.*—

R. —*Me too! Smiley face emoji. J.*—

As Jack pulled up to Rebecca's house, he noticed the familiar white super-duty truck in the driveway. As he climbed out of his own truck, he muttered under his breath, "What the hell is he doing here?" Jack's dog,

Keeper, came bounding from around the back of the house, tail wagging, sniffed at Jack's pants, and spent considerable time sniffing out Jack's wound. "Hey, Keep, there's my boy. I missed you." Jack gave Keep's body the once over from head to toe and kissed the side of Keep's face. Max and Manny, barking from the backyard, bounded around the corner and made a hasty beeline for Jack, both stopping to take a sniff at his leg. "Hey there, you two, thanks for taking care of Keep for me." He bent over to give Max and Manny a quick pat and looked up in time to see Rebecca crossing the yard to him.

"They all missed you, so did I." She leaned in and softly planted a kiss on his lips.

"You're a sight for sore eyes." He pulled her in tight and spied his father coming around the side of the house.

"Dad, what are you doing out here?" Jack said, eyeing his father suspiciously.

"It should be pretty obvious, Son." Henry hooked a thumb around his Carhartt coveralls completely covered in soot. "Jeb and I are out back setting up the ladder, we're cleaning out the chimney and wood stove. Rebecca is going to need a clean chimney and wood stove for those cool September nights."

"Dad, I told you, I'd get to it. We still have two weeks left in August."

"Son, you seemed to forget, it's Corcoran and Sons. I'm only semi-retired, and you just got out of the hospital with a bum leg. You need to heal. Focus on getting your energy back. Plus, you still have to wrap up Cal's place. I'm going to be out here, helping out, so get used to it!"

Jack grimaced as his father, chimney broom in hand, head toward the side yard, and he knew he'd been put in his place by the old man. There was no arguing with his father when he laid down the law.

Rebecca raised her eyebrows and shrugged.

"He's great. He reminds me of someone I know."

"Yeah, but he's a stubborn old man who refuses to let me take the reins. He's been 'semi-retired' for the past ten years. My dad will work until the day he keels over, but, I guess, he'll go doing something he loves. You smell great by the way."

"Must be the maple syrup. Your dad brought two dozen maple donuts with him from the Sugar Shack. I'm in heaven."

"My dad and his maple donuts. My mom would kill him if she knew."

Jack winced and rubbed his leg. He let out a long breath.

"Let's get you off the leg. How about I make us some fresh coffee to go with the donuts?"

"I'm in. The hospital coffee was awful." Jack sat at the table and ran a hand over the wood before grabbing a donut.

Rebecca set the large mug of coffee in front of Jack, who already was busy working on his second donut.

"Thanks," he said. He ran a finger under her eye. "Are you having trouble sleeping?"

"I am. I've been dreaming a lot lately, and when I'm not dreaming, I'm tossing and turning. Today, the coffee is a godsend."

He reached over and stroked her arm.

"I'm thinking we both could use some time

together. Maybe we could find a way to ditch those two?" He motioned out the window to where his father and Jeb were working hard trying to adjust the ladder on the roof and laughed as it dropped to the ground.

"How about after lunch we send them packing?"

"From the looks of it, they'll welcome the break," Jack said as he grabbed a third donut.

"Like father, like son?" Rebecca shot him an exaggerated look, as he smiled and took a huge bite.

"Hey, I just got out of the hospital. You heard what my dad said. I need to build my energy up, especially when I think of what I'm going to do to you later." He gave her a seductive wink.

"Jack, are you sure you're up to it? I can see the pain in your eyes from the injury."

"Believe me, every minute I spent in the hospital, all I thought about was you. Your visit was unforgettable. You were, by far, the best medicine ever." He held her hand.

"What was the best medicine, son?" Jack's father Henry entered the kitchen.

"Rebecca's cooking, she's a fine cook, Dad, very spicy."

"I love spicy food myself, Rebecca."

Rebecca choked slightly on her coffee and rose to gather the plates from the table. From the sink, she turned and shook her head at Jack and smiled back at Henry.

"Henry, pay no attention to your son. He's had too much sugar."

"Sorry, Dad, inside joke." Jack smiled.

"Okay, you two, there better be some donuts left?"

Chapter 21

Finally alone, with Jeb and his father well-fed and packed up, Jack took his time looking at her. His brown eyes bore a hole straight into hers as he skimmed his lips lightly over hers. His gaze shifted to her breasts, and her nipples hardened under his stare. He curled a finger around a loose strand of her hair, gave it a gentle pull as he met her lips again with his own. He let his hand dance across her collarbone, outlining the shape with his fingertips.

He studied her body like a man who, for the first time, was exploring new territory that he was set to claim for himself. He wanted to take his time with her, slowly, inch by beautiful inch. He bent down and kissed her neck, followed the same path across her collarbone he used with his hands. Each tender kiss sending pulsing waves of electricity straight from him and through her.

With a sweet smile, he gazed down at her and cupped a hand to her breast, kneading it softly as he lowered his mouth to hers. When he felt her hands on him, he took her hands and placed them by her side. "Wait," he whispered, "just let me touch you for a while. I've dreamed of this."

"But Jack…" Her words stopped as his lips covered her mouth.

He trailed his fingers slowly down her shoulders

along each of her arms and felt the eruption of goosebumps as they formed under his tender touch. He ended at her hands, held and squeezed as his eyes smiled into hers. He pulled her to him and allowed his hands to roam up and down, feeling the soft contours of her back. Leaning down, he pressed his lips against her mouth, his tongue passionately searching, and then, he heard the soft moan escape her throat.

The power of the kiss coursed through his body, like the taste and warmth of a sip of fine whiskey, aged to perfection. *My God*, he thought, *please don't ever let this ever end*. The wave of emotion was so powerful and so intense that when it hit him, it risked knocking the air right out of him. *I'm falling hard.*

He tried to empty his head and just let his hands do the talking and the feeling. He was breathless. Her surrender to him inflamed his own desire. His heart swelled again with emotion as she peered into his eyes. Eyes locked on each other, he laced his fingers under the soft pink camisole she wore. The delicate lace was all that separated him from her, and he released it from her shoulders. "You're so beautiful." He bowed her body toward his touch, toward the feeling of each of his fingertips as they caressed and felt as her body trembled. He was aware of her need, the intensity building, and let his fingers match her need.

"Jack, please," she begged.

His heart melted when she spoke, and he brushed his lips over each breast before taking a nipple between his lips. He felt the hot pulse of her skin hum as his mouth and hands devoured and feasted.

****

Rebecca heard herself gasp with desire, with need,

and she pulled his head closer to her breast. As he ravished her breasts, her thighs tensed until she couldn't help but rub them together. Her craving for him built with each brush of his mouth against her nipples. She wanted, no, she needed him to claim her. Her body was hot and ready to have him inside her. She welcomed his fingers as they fell between her legs, opened for him as he caressed her, his breath hot on her neck.

Kneeling in front of her, he removed her lace and replaced his fingers with his mouth delighting in the scent of her. She whimpered and placed her hands in his hair to guide him. Her heart raced, every one of her cells in her body quivering just waiting to explode. Her entire body was racked with sensation. She tried to hold back, until, at last, she cried out, feeling the gentle kisses he placed, in the end, on each of her thighs. The aftershock of her orgasm rocked both of them as he picked her up. *The man was a genius in bed. Definitely, gifted.*

"Jack, please be careful with your leg."

"Believe me, I'd be willing to lose this leg if it meant I could stay with you in this bed forever. I'm okay, I'm better than okay," he said as he placed her on the bed.

As she watched him undress, first his belt, and then his jeans, her body trembled again with excitement. The bandage on his leg was secured as he removed his boxers. Lowering himself to the bed, she felt his head rest on her breast and him hard against her. "Can I stay between your breasts forever?" he asked, nuzzling her close.

She laughed and shifted her body over him, careful not to put her weight on his wound.

"My turn, Jack. I want to feel every inch of you." With her hands, she explored his broad shoulders, played with the hint of dark hair on his chest, and traced around a scar on his left bicep.

"Another run-in with a tree?"

"Very funny! No, this time it was a baseball injury from high school."

"Baseball, huh? Very sexy."

She bent and gently kissed it. Jack started to shift her hips, and she gently pushed him down.

"Not yet, I'm still exploring."

"You're killing me." He groaned.

She kissed his chest, trailed kisses down his long torso so she could take him in her mouth. She used her lips and tongue, exploring him inch by inch, running her tongue down the length of him. On a moan, she took him in deeper with a little bite.

"I want to make you lose control," she whispered.

Hearing his desire inflamed her own, driving her to take him deeper yet. Her control over him was intoxicating. She heard him call out her name with urgency as she felt his hands on her helping to guide her mouth. He was close. She lifted her head, gave him a sly smile as she rose to straddle him and set the pace for the two of them. Thrusting her hips, slowly at first, wanting to feel him in her depths. Satisfied, she quickened the pace and felt her own orgasm building.

With his hands on her hips, and his fingertips pressing into each side, he helped guide her deeper. She let him set the pace, and with powerful thrusts, every inch of her was rocked. She arched her back, clenched him tight, and with one last shudder, the sound of their love, the harmony of two souls coming together filled the room. She collapsed on him and shivered at his touch, riding the last waves of her orgasm. She molded her body to his, heard him utter a "Wow" under his breath, and smiled to herself.

"You can say that again, Jack Corcoran."

He laughed and pulled her closer. "I can say one thing, Rebecca McCabe, you are thorough."

She stretched like a lazy cat and sat up.

"You're by far the sexiest woman I've ever known."

"Sexy and hungry!"

He laughed a huge laugh which made her face beam.

"You laugh, but I am! That was quite the workout."

"Now you mention it, I could eat." He flopped back against the pillows. "Great bed, by the way, excellent springs."

She grabbed his Corcoran and Sons T-shirt off the bedpost and shimmied it over her body with the hem of the shirt falling at mid-thigh. She smiled as Lulu jumped on the bed and kneaded the covers.

"Jesus, I don't think I've ever seen anyone wear that T-shirt better. I think Corcoran and Sons would get a lot more work if we advertised you wearing that shirt. I can't get enough of you."

The dimple on her face deepened. "Well, you're going to have to. Pizza's calling, besides Lulu wants some loving," she said and headed downstairs.

In the kitchen, she turned on her music and danced, her body energized. For the first time in a long time, she was not only sexually satisfied by a man she liked but also one she found sexy as hell. And in return, she felt sexy and happy. With all three dogs snuggled together under the kitchen table, she bent down to give each a rub. "You guys look comfy." They all shot her a look—one of neglect—and she added, "Who wants a treat?"

Chapter 22

After doling out the puppy cookies, she opened the fridge, took out the leftover pizza, beer, and arugula salad from yesterday. She heated up the oven and set the pizza to warm. She opened two bottles of Long Trail beer and placed them on the table. Yes, she thought, it's been a long dry trail, but thinking about Jack, it was all changing for the better. It was worth the wait.

She grabbed some placemats and plates from the cupboard. She started to set the beautiful old wooden table in the middle of the kitchen—the table handed down to her from her grandparents. The imperfections, each nick and patch of finish worn off, had a story. The old table reflected a history of countless family meals, celebrations, kids sitting after dinner finishing homework with tears, and laughter. She ran her hand across the surface of the old wood. *Maybe someday, my kids, my family*, and for the first time, she let herself believe it could happen.

The goosebumps ran up her arms, a cold draft circled her body as the lights above her head flickered. The image floated before her eyes. In the corner of the kitchen by the fireplace, sat a little child with blonde hair, humming a tune and playing with a doll. The girl's mother sat next to her in a rocking chair, mending a piece of cloth. The woman met Rebecca's eyes, and she smiled. Max came and sat at Rebecca's side, stared at the fireplace, and started to whine.

"Hush, Maxie, it's okay."

The woman in the rocking chair turned and smiled at Max.

"Max, I think she likes you." Rebecca gave her dog's head a quick stroke. Glancing back toward the fireplace, the image had disappeared.

She turned to find Jack standing in the doorway. With Patsy Cline blaring from the kitchen speakers, she moved to him, wrapped her arms around him and, together, they swayed to the music.

"What are you thinking about?" he asked.

"Oh, a lot, but mostly just you and how sturdy this beautiful table looks." She turned to face him, took his face in her hands, and kissed him slowly and with intent, like a woman starving for more, a lot more.

"I like how you think."

She laughed as he rounded her bottom, lifted, and eased her up onto the table, slowly taking her lower lip between his teeth for a soft nip. He gathered his T-shirt in his hands and pulled it off over her head. He sighed at the look of her, kissed the freckles on her nose that he found incredibly alluring.

"Should we check out how sturdy the table really is?" he whispered in her ear.

Rebecca leaned in so he could trace his mouth over her neck, while her hands outlined the hard muscles of his back. Feeling the heat grow, she drew him in.

"I'm taking that as a yes," Jack said as he leaned her body back.

After a sweaty round two, they made dinner together. He tossed the leftover salad as she lifted the pizza from the oven. He thought to himself, how she filled the empty parts of him, the parts he let die off after Alice and Cam tore him to pieces with betrayal. Parts of his heart were slowly coming back, nurtured by her goodness, her love, and her strength. Rebecca was a woman who lived her life with integrity, which mattered to him. Alice and Cam could no longer hurt him, he could let the anger go. What was the saying, the best revenge is to love well. Jack hoped that in Rebecca, that's what he'd found, love.

****

She wrapped her arms around him and hugged him from behind, laying her cheek against his back. She felt his warmth and the hard planes of his back. With the dogs sprawled out on the kitchen floor and the aroma of pizza filling the air. *It was perfect.* Grabbing napkins, she finished setting the table. She thought to herself, *Like the table, Jack is sturdy. I want, no, I need sturdy in my life.* Setting down the napkin next to his plate she leaned down and kissed his cheek.

"Rebecca, I need to ask you a question."

"Sure, anything," she said as she placed the plate of pizza before him.

"I wanted to ask you if you would like to go to my buddy Peter's Labor Day Party with me?"

"You mean like a real date?" she teased.

"Yes, like a real date. Peter and his partner, Tom Attwell, own the Crescent Inn on Main Street. They throw a hell of a party."

"Sounds like fun. I would love to go."

"Wait until you get a load of the inn. It was a dream job for Corcoran and Sons. We helped Peter and Tom restore it."

"I met Tom at the Eden Library. Nice guy."

"Tom's a great guy. Peter and I grew up together, we're tight. Peter and Tom have been together for years."

"I also met Carol, his assistant. She's lovely. She's going to help me with a research project."

"Carol is also a good friend of mine. And don't let her librarian outfits fool you—she definitely has a wild side and a heart of gold."

"Carol? A wild side? Really? I never would've guessed by looking at her."

"So, a research project huh? Going to fill me in?" he said, taking a big bite of pizza.

"Maybe if you play your cards right."

"Oh, I'll play my cards right." He leaned over, found her sweet spot, and trailed the tenderest of kisses down her neck.

"Yep, that definitely works."

"Okay, then spill it."

"I'm actually researching the history of this house, past owners, land use. I'm interested in knowing the history, who and what came before me. Like reading a book, I want to know the chapters that came before me." She rose, moved to the fridge, grabbed another beer, and motioned to Jack with the bottle. "Do you want another?"

"I'd love another."

She snapped off the top and handed him the beer. "This house is filled with rich details, every nook and cranny tells a story, and I want to know what that story is," she mused.

"A place like this I'm sure has a rich history. I know the Parkers loved this house and the land, raised a small brood here. They lived here for as long as I can remember."

"I am going all the way back, to the beginning, to when the house was built, starting with the original owners who built the house in 1820."

"That sounds like quite the undertaking."

"The first time I stepped into this house, onto this land, I felt at home. Don't get me wrong, there's an intensity here. Actually, that was part of the reason I was attracted to it. A home that comes with its own history, its own secrets just waiting to be uncovered. I want to understand its past and how it might or might not be impacting the present. I have to tell you I'm excited about this project."

"It does sound interesting. You'll get a chance to talk to the Parkers at Peter's party. Let me know if there is anything I can do to help."

"I will. Thanks, but right now I need help with just one thing," she said, squeezing his forearm.

"Oh, Rebecca, you might need to give me an hour. I'm so full, I don't think I can move."

She chuckled. "No, Jack, I meant the dishes."

"Oh, of course, but then I need to get a couple of hours of work done, priming the ceiling in the living room. I don't want to give my father any more excuses to be out here."

"Perfect. While you're busy priming I have a couple of deadlines to meet."

After the dishes were done, Jack set the ladder up, opened the window to get some fresh air flowing, and switched on his favorite playlist on his cellphone. He hated to admit it, but a part of him was disappointed that she was talking about doing the dishes instead of doing each other. Plenty of work to do, only thing was, he wasn't up for working, especially knowing she was a room away. His heart and his mind were turned upside down, and it was a great feeling.

He blew out a breath, picked up the paintbrush, and got to work.

He glanced down to find her watching him from the doorway. "How's the work going?" he asked, swiping at the ceiling with the brush.

She cocked an eye at him. "It's impossible to focus when my mind keeps thinking about your arms around me and you inside…"

"You're killing me, Rebecca." Giving into the yearning, he climbed down the ladder, circled her body, and touched his lips to hers. "Let's go to bed."

Chapter 23

The next day, Rebecca set the stove to warm and checked the clock. If she were quick, she'd have enough time to video chat with her mom before Carol arrived. She was bursting to tell her mom all about Jack and how for the first time she believed her dreams of finding lasting love could come true. Pouring a glass of iced tea, she grabbed her phone, curled up in her favorite chair, and waited for her mom to answer. Her niece, Olivia, filled the screen.

"Auntie Becca!" Olivia screamed gleefully.

"Did you take Grandma's phone again?" Rebecca jokingly accused as her niece erupted into giggles. "Where's Grandma?"

"Grandma's making lunch."

Rebecca heard her mother's voice yelling over the chaos.

"Grandma said she'd call you back later. Hey…" Olivia protested as Rebecca's brother Rory's face filled the screen.

Rebecca laughed as her brother tried to negotiate with his daughter.

"Olivia, I promise you can talk more after I say hello to Auntie Becca," he said firmly and turned his face into the screen.

"Remind me why I had kids again?"

"Because you love them, Rory."

"Oh, that's right, now I remember. How is my favorite sister doing? And why the hell haven't you texted?" Rory demanded.

Rebecca saw the familiar strain of worry cross his face. "I'm sorry! You do realize I'm a grown woman, right? And, for the record, I'm your only sister."

"You'll always be the baby, and I'll always be the big brother. When can I come up?"

"You're just not going to rest until you inspect my new digs. Am I right?"

"Damn straight. Sean and I are wondering if a weekend at the end of September works? Just us, no kids so we have time to help with any home repairs."

"I actually hired someone to help with the repairs."

"You what?! How do you know if they're any good? Wait until I tell dad and Sean."

Rebecca heard the knock at the door, dogs barking, a cat meowing, and gave her dogs the command to be quiet.

"Rory, I'll have to call you back. Someone is at the door."

"Who's at the door?" he demanded.

"Seriously, Rory? You need to take up a new cause."

"Not in this lifetime, Sister, and we're not done talking about this repair person."

"Whatever! I love you, brother."

"I love you too, Becca. Wait, hold on…Mom just yelled she'll call you back later."

"Great, talk to you guys soon. Bye, Rory."

"Bye, Sis."

Rebecca poked her head out of the kitchen to find Carol peering through the screened door.

"Hi, Carol, come on in."

"I thought I heard voices."

"I just got off the phone with my brother Rory."

"Oh, I'm sorry to interrupt. I'm a bit early."

"No problem. Everything is set up in the kitchen. I hope you like jerk chicken. I made it last night on the grill along with Jamaican peas and rice. Come on back. What can I get you to drink?"

"Water's fine," she said, stooping to pet Lulu, who was winding her way back and forth around her legs.

"That's Lulu, she's an attention whore."

"Aren't we all. She's sweet. And who are these two big guys?" Carol said reaching down to give the dogs a good rub.

"My two protectors—Maxie, the one with the red collar, and Manny, the green."

"I can see why you call them protectors. I wouldn't want to meet you two in a dark alley."

"Both have hearts of gold unless, of course, anyone tries to harm me. Then all bets are off."

"I'll keep that in mind. Wow, it really smells delicious in here. I love what you've done with the place. I love the wall color. Pale yellow just screams happy. The Parkers always kept it so dark. Now it looks bright and homey. Love the pillows and candle holders too. Let me guess, Tender Moments in town?"

"Yes, the owner, Melissa, was so helpful. She knew exactly what I was going for."

"Melissa has a good eye. Your place is really coming together."

"Thank you, there is still so much to get done, but I do feel at home in this old house. I love it." Rebecca handed Carol a plate. "There is also some salad here.

Help yourself."

As Carol filled her plate, she eyed Rebecca. "So, the whole town is talking about you and Jack Corcoran."

Rebecca stopped, holding the chicken plate mid-air, shocked. "Sure you don't want to try the chicken first?"

Carol tossed her head back and laughed. "I'm just the messenger."

"Oh Lord, well, that got out fast."

"One thing about a small town is we all love to gossip."

"I'm, umm…clearly new to small-town living," Rebecca said, fumbling for words.

"Well, Tom and I were talking at the library about it, and we both are thrilled. Jack is a good friend of ours." Hopeful, Carol searched Rebecca's face, looking for dirt.

"You and Tom? Talking at the…the…library?" she said, flustered.

"Tom and I spend a lot, and I mean a lot, of time together. He's my best friend and, well, we love to talk about what's new in town. Like it or not, currently, you and Jack are big news," Carol said as she shrugged.

"I guess that makes sense. It's very new—don't get me wrong, I'm loving every minute of it—but I don't think my head has caught up with my heart. I fell hard for Jack."

"Tom is going to flip! Tom's partner Peter is one of Jack's best friends. Tom's been working Peter over trying to get the scoop, but Peter refuses to dish."

"Peter sounds like a loyal friend."

"Yeah, yeah but it's been driving Tom and me

118

crazy. There's no denying Jack is good looking, God, when I see him in those Carhatts around town, seriously great butt."

"No argument, here."

"He's also a great guy. His whole family is great, they really are a huge part of the fabric of this town. The whole town loves the Corcoran family."

Heeding Carol's words, Rebecca received the message loud and clear. The warning not to hurt one of their own. Rebecca was the outsider. She had no intention of hurting Jack but also knew it was early in their relationship. "Carol, I can honestly say I have never felt what I am feeling with Jack before, not with anyone. Jack is different. I'm just letting my heart and body enjoy it. Believe me, it was a long dry spell before Jack." Rebecca saw the expression of longing on Carol's face and knew all too well the feeling. "How about you? Are you dating anyone? If you don't mind me asking."

"No, not for a while," Carol replied.

"How come?"

"Well." She hesitated, gathering her words carefully. "I was dating this guy, a CPA, in Morrisville for a couple of years, but it didn't work out."

Rebecca felt the ache hit her heart with force, and knew she was picking up Carol's pain. Rebecca knew this man had hurt Carol deeply and she was having difficulty healing from the loss.

"How long ago was it?"

"Umm, it was about three years ago. I know it's crazy to still be pining for him, but here I am. Crazy and pathetic as it is."

"It sounds hard."

"Yup. I saw on social media he recently had a baby with the woman he dated after me."

Rebecca put her fork down and met Carol's eyes.

"Carol, you're not still…?"

"I know, I know, I'm a masochist, yes, I'm still friends with him on his social media page."

"Learning he had a baby must have hurt."

"It threw me for a loop. It actually felt like we were breaking up all over again. The last nail in the coffin. Now he has a family, and I sit here with all these feelings. I know I should be happy for him, but it hurts," Carol said.

"Why should you be happy for him? He broke your heart."

"You're right and, as stupid as it sounds, I'm still in love with him."

"Have you tried dating?"

"I did try online dating, even some of the more questionable sites, for about six months, but it was a disaster. The last guy I had a date with actually sent me a dick pic after."

"I hope for the both of you it was worth the data charges."

"It most certainly wasn't, if you get my drift. Tom and Peter are always trying to set me up, but I just don't feel ready."

Rebecca nodded knowingly.

"Carol, the first couple of years I was in Burlington I thought I was in love with this man, Ethan. He always wanted all my time and attention, but he didn't really want me. It was excruciating because I thought I was in love with him. I was young and completely inexperienced and alone. I let myself be used by him emotionally. He needed me but didn't want me."

"What did you do?"

"Initially, I thought I could change his mind. You know, work harder for him to fall in love with me. Show him how essential I was in his life. I lost myself. His interests became my interests. I didn't know who I was anymore."

"Been there, done that."

"After the heartbreak, and it did feel like my heart was literally breaking, I avoided dating for a long time until my mom said to me, 'If you don't get back on the horse, you will never learn to love.' I got the message. It wasn't easy to do, but she was right. I started to date again. I, too, tried the online thing. Like you, I had my share of loser dates, but I had to put my heart out there again. Believe me, it was better than sitting home alone and wallowing in the pain."

"I know you're right, but I'm not sure my heart can take much more."

"That's why women have each other and wine."

"Thank God for that!"

"You said it. Okay, enough of men, so the plan is to finish lunch and head south to Barre."

"Yes, oh, I almost forgot to mention, I have some news to share." Carol's face lit up like she just won the lottery. "I spoke with my friend, Megan Allen, who is the head librarian at the Vermont Historical Society, she located a number of diaries starting in the 1780s to 1870s from women who lived in Eden. One of the authors, in particular, was an incredibly prolific writer, a Ms. Hattie Cleveland. She started her journal in 1820 and wrote every day for fifty years. Hattie was born and raised in Eden, a spinster who took care of the family farm with her three bachelor brothers. I think we start with the town's history, review the property deeds, and then move on to the Vermont vital records. If we have time we can dive into the diaries. If we run out of time or energy, Megan can email us the PDFs of the complete diary. Megan also mentioned another diary written by Cyrene Winters."

"Winters, like Cam Winters?" Rebecca asked.

"Exactly, the Winters are one of the founding families in Eden. Although, Megan said the diary of Cyrene Winters is incomplete, containing only a couple of entries about the family farm. It's not going to tell us much."

"Carol, what do you hope to gain from the diaries?"

"Often diaries contain accounts of what is happening in the community, personal reflections, and sometimes, even gossip. Research is like a good mystery. You never know what you will find."

Chapter 24

After two hours, Rebecca stood, rolled her shoulders to release the tension, and shut the book on the history of Eden. "I need a break," she said idly.

"Yeah, me too," Carol said, standing and stretching.

They both looked up to find Megan Allen approaching, notebook in hand.

"I wanted to check in with you both before I go on break to see if you need anything or have any questions?"

"Megan, I am wondering if you would pull the Vermont Vital Records for the early Nineteenth Century for Eden. I think we're done with the books on the settlement of Eden, riveting as they were," Carol joked.

"Sure, I can do that for you. I will leave the box containing the vital records and the reference slips on the cart next to your table."

"Perfect, thank you, Megan."

"Is there a water fountain close by?" Rebecca asked, grabbing her empty water bottle from the table.

"Good idea. I could use some water. Pretty dry material up to this point. No pun intended."

"Water fountain is through the double doors to the right, ladies."

When they stepped into the hallway, Carol turned

to her. "Hard life, clearing land, families moving in on the hope to start farming, especially clearing boulders out of the fields by hand, brutal work."

"I know. I'm not sure I would've survived it."

She'd always found researching tedious but necessary work and was thankful to have Carol by her side.

Back at the table, Rebecca studied the box Megan had left. She knew in her heart and head the information she was looking for was in this box. Hesitation crept through her. Rebecca caught the glimpse of a young woman holding the hand of a small child as they walked on the sidewalk out front. From her experience, the universe provided information and often clues if one was paying attention. Rebecca learned not to discount any of it.

"Rebecca?"

"Yes, sorry, what is it?"

"According to this, the house was built for Reverend Hiram Winters in 1820." Carol opened her notebook and started to type in a timeline.

"Winters again?"

"I would bet a relative of Cam's."

"That's curious. Cam sold me the house but never mentioned a relative of his built the house. Do you find that odd that he never mentioned that his family originally built the house?"

"Well, it's possible he didn't know the entire history of the house."

"True," Rebecca considered.

"Can you grab the Vital Records to see if there is an account of Reverend Winters?"

Rebecca opened the file, happy to be guided in this

process by Carol, and scanned through the log. "Here's one," Rebecca said as she read out loud from the page. "Married, in Eden, Vermont, Reverend Hiram Winters and Miss Polly Demers, on March 4, 1831. Demers, I remember the name from the settlement of Eden book."

"Yes, Demers is another one of the founding families in Eden. The Demers family were dairy farmers who came down from Canada. Mainly dairy, and, I also believe, apples. A number of Demers still farm even today. There is a longstanding feud between the Demers and the Winters. I'm not sure the background of the feud or why it continues. Okay, keep going, any other account of Hiram or Polly?"

"Yes, here's another, a birth announcement, sweet, a baby girl," Rebecca smiled at the thought of the baby. "Birth, in Eden, Vermont, daughter Silence to Reverend Hiram Winters and Polly Winters, January 29, 1832." A snapshot of an exhausted mother cradling a baby formed in Rebecca's head.

"Okay, to summarize, we have Reverend Winters who built the house, his marriage to Polly Demers, and now the birth of their first child, Silence. Any other record of more children for Hiram and Polly?" Carol queried.

"No, not yet, not that I see. Oh, wait, here we go. Oh my, how sad, drowned, in Eden, Vermont, Polly Winters, age 22, wife of Reverend Hiram Winters, on July 4, 1836."

"Drowned? That is sad, and so young."

Sorrow filled Rebecca's chest. She envisioned the young mother dead on the bank of the pond, clutching her child to her breast.

"Rebecca, you look like you've seen a ghost. Are

you okay?"

"I'm okay, but here's another entry, drowned, in Eden, Vermont, Miss Silence Winters, age 4, daughter of Reverend Hiram Winters and Polly Winters, on July 4th, 1836."

As Rebecca read, she heard a mother in despair, screaming, and saw the image of a child drowning. The child's eyes filled with terror as they peered through the surface of the water pleading for air. Rebecca let the energy flow through her, allowing it to slowly form and dissipate. Trying to hold onto the image was useless. She closed her eyes for a moment.

"Rebecca?"

"Sorry, it's just so tragic."

"I'm only speculating, but I wonder if Polly was trying to save her child from drowning?"

"What makes you think that?"

"I know saving a drowning victim can be difficult and puts the person who is attempting to rescue in danger," Carol mused. "I wonder if Polly went in the water to save her daughter. Maybe she became overwhelmed, panicked, and then they both ended up drowning."

"It's certainly possible." Rebecca sat quietly. She thought of the child's giggling and the image of the small girl playing in front of the fireplace in her kitchen. *Could it be the spirit occupying my house is the little girl, Silence Winters*? Rebecca thought of the first day, the drive to her new home, spying the little girl, wet from a swim, and she vowed to find out the truth.

Carol rose, beginning to pace. "Okay, so far we know Reverend Winters built the house." She stopped and rested her hands on the table. "He married Polly

Demers, they had one child, a girl Silence, and the Reverend Winters lost both his wife and daughter in 1836 to drowning. What we don't know is if the drownings occurred on your property."

"You mean in the pond out back," Rebecca said, not needing a book to tell her what she already knew in her heart. Polly and Silence drowned in the pond out back.

"I think we should move on to Hattie Cleveland's diaries. I'll ask Megan to highlight all diary entries containing a reference to any of the Winters or Demers families," Carol said. "The diaries covered the same period when the Winters occupied the house, and I'm guessing she would have mentioned the drownings. A mother and child drowning would've been big news in a rural community. It would be big news today. According to this map of 1820, the Cleveland farm was the closest farm to the Winters' family home, so I'm guessing that Hattie wrote about it."

Rebecca picked up the file and scanned it with her eyes. "Carol," she said, "listen to this: The Reverend Winters, died, at Eden, Vermont, age 47. Thrown from horse, dragged by foot 30 yards. Died four days later on November 14, 1836. A witness and neighbor of Reverend Winters said he thinks a sound spooked the horse, causing the Reverend to be thrown." She gave her a long look as she thought. Behind Carol's head, standing by the window, she saw them—a man dressed in all black, his hands firmly placed on the shoulders of a small girl and a woman.

Rebecca laid her head down on the cold surface of the table—the weariness from the sadness of the records left a throbbing in her temple. She pressed her fingers against her eyes, holding pressure to release the vibration that took hold. When she turned back, they were gone.

"This isn't what I ever imagined we'd find," Carol mused.

Rebecca knew in her heart there was sadness and grief. Now she believed there was violence.

"It's a lot of information to take in and so very sad," Carol said. "I'm going to talk to Megan about cross-checking the dates now with Hattie Cleveland's diaries." Carol left Rebecca siting alone with her thoughts at the long table.

"Here we go," Carol said, handing the thick file to Rebecca.

Rebecca opened the file and, with care, leafed through the copied pages of the worn diary entries. The edges of the copied pages were smeared with black ink, and Rebecca visualized Hattie sitting at her writing desk. Hattie's full skirt billowed out from under the desk as she wrote. Her hands smudged with ink as she dipped her pen in a decorative glass bottle, going about her daily routine of documenting her day.

"September 20th, 1820. Had a pleasant talk with my brother Fitch who talked of Reverend Winters' home being almost complete. The Reverend's family owns the large dairy farm on East Hill Rd., the family is a pious bunch but not overly sociable, keep to themselves. Reverend Hiram Winters is the oldest of the clan with two brothers and one sister. The Reverend's father, John, was said to be a hard worker but mean-spirited before his untimely death. When May Bouchard visited this evening, she gossiped about the family and said that when John Winters was alive, he would fly

into such passions, beating his children senseless. Not much is known of his mother, Cyrene. When the Reverend moves in, I will go over with an apple pie to welcome him and bring one of my brothers over to accompany me."

"October 3rd, 1820. It has been a day of such beauty, the air pure, and the mountains so full of color, crimson, yellows, oranges. Made a call with my brother Henry to welcome the Reverend Winters to his new home. Reverend spoke of erecting a meeting house to preach from, possibly land on East Hill given to him by his mother. He asked for Henry and me to pray with him. Reverend Winters spoke with pride that he hath pleased a merciful God with his strong, unwavering faith, he seemed to be taken over by spirit and in a harsh voice proclaimed, "What must I do to be saved?" His face looked consumed with anger, feeling uneasy I excused myself stating Henry and I needed to get back to the farm so I could start the cooking. As Henry and I took leave, Henry made a comment that he thought the Reverend an odd man. My nerves were high for the rest of the night."

"July 21st, 1825. The sun is scorching hot. I took tea with my brother Henry who needed a break from the field. Henry said he ran into the Reverend Winters and the woman he is courting, a Miss Louisa Ann Putnam from Middlesex in town earlier today. Henry said she is a lovely young woman from a well-established farming family."

"March 29th, 1826. Fitch came home from the feed store sullen over the talk in town about the Reverend Winters. The poor man is grieving the loss of his fiancée Louisa Ann Putnam. Poor young Louisa

Putnam was found dead last week, frozen on the bank of the Winooski. Fitch said it appeared one of Louisa's boots became lodged between two rocks, she fell, hit her head, and froze to death. A most tragic ending for such a fine young woman. I paused to think what on earth was she doing this time of year along the river. Tobias Anderson told Fitch that Reverend Winters was the last to see her alive. The rumor is he met her at the Winooski River Bridge to talk about wedding plans and after they parted ways. Conjecture is she took the shortcut along the river to get home. Tobias said some of the townspeople are gossiping saying Louisa Putnam was breaking off her engagement because of her station and the Reverend's want of money. Fitch said the Putnam family will have a public mourning at the house, but the Reverend is too ill to attend."

As Carol listened to Rebecca read from the diary, the image of Louisa and the Reverend on the bridge played in her head. Louisa comforting the young man. Her gloved hand on his in an attempt to ease the blow.

"April 12th, 1826. My brothers John and Fitch accompanied me to the Reverend Winters' home to drop off a venison meat pie. The Reverend's mother, Cyrene, welcomed us at the door and invited us to join her for tea. Over tea she explained she is caring for her son who is in deep mourning over the loss of his sweet Louisa. Cyrene Winters said the oddest thing during tea. She said she didn't like to speak ill of the dead but, in her opinion, Louisa Putnam was a headstrong young woman who didn't know how to hold her tongue. She went on to say that it was only through death that Louisa learned a valuable lesson. My brothers and I finished our tea quickly and took leave. I fear Cyrene

Winters is quite mad."

"May 7th, 1831. My brothers and I were invited to attend the Reverend Winters' wedding ceremony at the old Meeting House. The weather was stifling hot for early May. Reverend Winters married Polly Demers with their families in attendance. Polly made a beautiful bride. She wore the most lovely ivory silk damask gown with leg-o'-mutton sleeves, a true sight. The Reverend wore a worn black plain suit, I thought most inappropriate for such an auspicious occasion. May Bouchard couldn't stop talking about the Reverend's tasteless wear and the significant age differences between the couple. Polly's bright smile was dampened by the Reverend's dour expression."

"August 10th, 1831. Invited Polly Winters over for tea. She seemed miserable but denied that she was feeling in any state. She seemed as nervous as a church mouse. She didn't touch any of the danishes that I put out. She stayed but an hour before heading back, stating that the "Reverend needed her home." I thought it odd that she refers to her husband as the 'Reverend.' I must make time to visit her more often."

"October 24th, 1831. Went to visit Polly Winters, who is with child. Polly had a large bruise covering her entire right eye. When I questioned her she said a branch caught her in the eye as she was walking the path to the pond. When Polly asked the Reverend to bring in more wood for the fire, the look he gave her made me shudder. Polly retrieved the wood herself even big with child. Reverend Winters said but two words to me and left abruptly. I think my brother Henry is right, the Reverend is an odd man. I have a good deal of curiosity about the carryings-on in the Winters' home."

"January 28th, 1832. Called out to the home of Reverend Winters, setting out in the most unforgiving snowstorms. Sheets of bone-chilling wet snow plummeted us on the journey. Brother Henry before us, lighting the way, as Fitch and I followed his light, illuminated, in the sleigh. Our horse fell, having difficulty staying on course. The horse, in a frantic state, reared until Fitch unhitched him. I walked the rest of the way through the heavy wet snow to the Winters, thanking God I was close to the Reverend's home. The snow has not stopped, and I fear I might get housebound. The wind is howling fiercely, and my nerves are high. Polly Winters is laboring. In attendance is the Reverend's sister Caroline and his mother, Cyrene. Polly was brave in her labors."

"January 29th, 1832. Polly gave birth to a strong big baby girl early, with the loudest wail I have ever heard. The snow has finally stopped, and the wind has died down. The Reverend proclaimed his daughter should be named Silence, a virtue he hopes she will possess. I put Polly to bed with her baby."

"October 4th, 1833. Called over to see Polly Winters who confided her husband has taken ill to his bed for the past week. Polly was in an agitated state trying to keep Silence quiet as not to upset the Reverend. I had an uneasy feeling being in the Winters house and was relieved to take leave."

"July 3rd, 1834. Ran into Sally Paul Demers who mentioned her worry for her daughter Polly and asked for prayers. I asked if Polly has taken ill but Sally said she was called out to Polly's house, and Polly was laid up with a broken limb. When I inquired about her granddaughter Silence, Sally Paul laughed, stating

Silence is anything but silent. She mentioned Silence is staying with her until Polly is up and around. She joked that at Silence's age her daughter Polly was scared of her own shadow. I am under the impression Sally Paul doesn't care too kindly for her son-in law, when I asked about the Reverend, she scoffed, called the Reverend a knave, and took leave."

"March 4th, 1836. Had a rather odd visit with Polly Winters who asked for my advice on what makes a child wicked. Not having children of my own I couldn't say and directed her to speak to her mother. She said her mother would be angry if she knew her husband was referring to their daughter Silence as a wicked child. She spoke of her husband's ill-tempered fits. Polly stated the Reverend proclaimed his daughter was the workings of the devil. I did try to ease Polly's mind and said Silence is an innocent lamb in God's eyes, just a child, and to pray. This seemed to bring some relief and Polly thanked me for my words."

"July 5th, 1836. A great tragedy has marked Reverend Winters' home. His wife and daughter drowned in the pond out back. A great sadness has fallen over Eden. Henry, Tom, and I went to pay our respects. Our brother Fitch refused to come with us, stating he has his reasons. When we arrived at the Reverend Winters' home we were told the Reverend has taken to his bed, his sister and brothers were at the house as well as his mother Cyrene. Polly's family was not at the home which I found odd. We brought smoked venison for the family and inquired about a service. No word was given."

Slivers of apprehension cut through Rebecca, and she stopped reading. Out of the corner of her eye, she caught the wispy shadow of a man in black, his head bowed in prayer.

"I need some fresh air. Can we take a break, Carol?"

"Of course, go get some air. I'll sit and finish up the timeline."

Rebecca stood and moved out onto the back porch. She leaned over the rail, felt the sun's warmth on her face, and breathed in the summer air. The faintest smell of sweet rosehips filled her nostrils, and she inhaled the earthy sweet scent deeply.

Carol opened the door and peeked out.

"Sorry to interrupt your break. Just checking in to see how you're doing?"

"Better, I couldn't breathe in there."

"I asked Megan to email us the PDF of Hattie's diary. I, for one, am done with the Winters family for today."

"You read my mind. Thanks, Carol."

"Are you ready to head in and get packed up?"

"Let's do it."

Back at the table, Rebecca and Carol stood silently and collected their things.

"You're all set, ladies. Enjoy the rest of your day," Megan said, waving.

"Thanks, Megan. You too!" Carol gave an audible wistful sigh as she watched Megan leave the room. "I have a total crush on Megan. A couple of weeks ago I had a sex dream about her. Very hot," she said, as Megan left the room.

When Rebecca roared with laughter, Carol attempted to hush her and glanced about the room, nervously.

"Sorry, sorry," Rebecca said, lowering her voice. "I forget we're in a library. I needed a good distraction, and you gave me one. Thank you for that."

"You're welcome. Are you ready to head back to Eden? On the way, I'll tell you all about my hot librarian dream."

"Oh, I can't wait to hear all about it. After all the sadness we just read, hearing about your sex dream would be a gift."

As they headed out to the car, Carol paused and leaned over the car hood. "Rebecca, I'm usually not one who listens to gossip, well except, of course, with Tom. Anyway, the Winters family has quite a long history of violence, alcoholism, and mental illness. You ask anyone who grew up in Eden about the Winters, and you'll hear a story. It's quite sad."

"Even Cam?" Rebecca asked.

"Oh yeah, Tom told me Cam was in and out of foster care for most of his life. The police were frequent flyers out at his house. Cam's father was known to be a violent drunk who beat him and his mother. It speaks to Cam's resilience that he's so successful and moved past growing up the way he did."

"I wonder how much Cam knows of his family's history?"

"I don't know. I've never heard Cam talk about his past. Granted, I was four grades behind all of them, but Jack and Peter were very tight with Cam growing up. In fact, Jack's parents often took Cam. Jack's parents were often Cam's foster parents. The State would always end up sending him back home. His father would vow never to drink again, well, until the next time. I think that's partly why I have such a soft spot for Cam."

"I can understand. You never really know what a person goes through, completely." Rebecca thought of her own childhood and how in one instant everything changed for her.

"Um, about that, Rebecca, I have a confession." Meeting her eyes, Rebecca waited. "I know about your past."

"You do? Did you research me?"

"No, nothing that extensive. I was curious about you. I suppose we're all a bit protective of Jack. So, I researched your name on the internet."

"Wow. I'm just a bit caught off guard. I don't know what to say."

"I know it probably seems like a complete invasion of privacy, but really it was part curiosity and part protecting my friend. I never realized I would hit on so much information. I didn't share any of it, not even with Tom."

"Well, I guess, I was just waiting for someone to ask me about it," Rebecca said reassuringly. "It's okay, Carol. It's part of who I am, it happened, there's no denying it. I am just one of many people who go through trauma and are lucky enough to survive it. It's the past."

"I appreciate you being so understanding. I want us to be friends, so I thought I should come clean."

"Thank you. I want us to be friends too, Carol, and, truthfully, part of me is relieved you know. It's one less person I have to explain my past to."

"You're one tough lady. I'm not sure I could've survived such an ordeal."

"You'd be surprised what you can get through. Like everyone, I have my moments of weakness, but I do take pride in my grit."

"I am confused, though, Rebecca. The article that ran in the Boston Globe about the abductions, there's a photo of you standing with a detective who said that without you he never would've been able to solve the case. That *you* were essential in saving that little girl. I'm curious how'd you save that girl? What did you do exactly?"

Rebecca shifted a little, away from Carol to hide her expression and gather her words.

Carol laid a hand on her arm. "It's okay if you're not ready to talk about it. I don't mean to pry, I'm curious that's all."

"I'll need wine to tell that story. When I'm ready, Carol, you'll be one of the first."

Chapter 25

On the drive back to Eden, Rebecca rested her eyes, her head pounding from the events of the day. She just wanted to get home and veg. Work on forgetting the contents of Hattie's diary that currently swirled in her head. When they reached Preston Road, the fog descended on the road like a heavy blanket, making driving near impossible. As Carol inched along, Rebecca saw the child standing by the stone wall. A man in black stood next to the child with a hand placed on the child's shoulder. Both figures were enveloped in the fog's wispy shadows. Rebecca turned back for another glimpse. "Did you see that, Carol?"

Carol pumped the car brake. "See what? Deer? A lot of deer out this time of year."

Rebecca rubbed her eyes. Maybe the fog was playing tricks on her. Seeing Jack's truck in her driveway had the pounding in her head easing up and her heart settling. She said goodbye to Carol and found Jack sitting on her front steps, a large pizza and a bottle of wine sitting alongside him.

"Jack, how'd you…?"

"Carol texted me about the research, said you both were feeling pretty weary. I thought maybe you could use some loving to shut it down. What's better than wine, pizza, and, maybe, a movie?"

"And you, it's perfect. Thank you. What movie

were you thinking?"

"I thought a night like tonight needed a strong female character. How about some kick-ass Katniss?"

"Perfect, right now, I need to tap into my inner female warrior."

After taking a hot shower, Rebecca found him upstairs in the spare room, where the TV and the oversized sofa ended up. He had lit candles and arranged the room for a movie night. On the coffee table sat a beautiful bouquet of wildflowers in one of her green-hued depression glass vases. A bottle of red wine with two wine glasses sat next to the flowers, along with a sausage and spinach pizza. The movie was cued up on the television.

"Jack, this is beyond perfect." She crossed the room to him, felt his strong arms embrace her, and thought to herself, *yes, beyond perfect.*

She ended up falling asleep with her head on his lap midway through the movie. She stirred as he placed her on the big four-poster bed. Half awake now, she reached out to him, to feel his warmth, the security of his arms, and take comfort.

She pulled him toward her onto the soft bed, felt his lips gently kissing her neck. His hands roamed to pull her nightshirt up and over her head, then found her full breasts. She sighed, shifted her body over his, her turn to drag his shirt over his head, her hands exploring the hard muscle and his body's firm planes.

Unbuckling his jeans, he guided her on, she set the pace, rocked slowly, freely, needed the quiet build up as she bent her head to kiss him. He thrust his hips one last time, as she cried out, feeling safe and loved. She released the pent-up sadness of the day, tears flowed, heart to heart, he held her as she sobbed until she fell back to sleep.

She didn't know what time it was when she woke from the dream, her chest pounding. In her dream, she was underwater, struggling to reach the surface. Above her, a face blurred peering down at hers. Cut off from air, knowing she was drowning, her hands grasped at the face above her for help. It disappeared from view, and she woke up.

Rebecca sat up in bed and glanced over at Jack. She listened to his light snoring and placed a hand on his heart to feel the comforting beat. Fully awake, she reached for her laptop, opened Hattie's diary, and began to read.

"July 6th, 1836. Fitch, Henry, and I went to the pond behind the Reverend's house to look at the place Polly and her daughter were found. We located the maple tree where it was reported Polly and Silence were laid after being pulled from the pond. It was said Polly still had a hold of her dead child in her arms. Even in death Polly was soothing her child. We walked around the bank by the maple tree. Holding hands, we gave a prayer up for Polly and her beautiful daughter, Silence. The scene at the pond was truly a beautiful sight and hard to believe such a tragedy occurred here. It gave me the most melancholy and nervous feeling within my heart."

"July 8th, 1836. Burial service for Polly Winters and daughter Silence who were laid to rest together. The Reverend from Cambridge came to conduct the sermon. The words in the sermon gave me pause, 'Wherefore let him that thinketh he standeth take heed lest he fall.' A sad day for all, I am weary and blue."

"August 10th, 1836. The District Attorney came calling to speak with my brother Fitch. This was startling as we have no idea why he came seeking Fitch. After he took leave, Fitch said the District Attorney came questioning him about the day Polly and her daughter Silence drowned. Fitch told the District Attorney he was in the woods that day scouting turkeys and he heard a great commotion. Fitch stated he heard what he thought was a bobcat, but thought it odd given it was daylight, he went investigating and saw Reverend Winters walking down the path away from the pond toward the house. Fitch said he thought the Reverend was angry, heard him mutter over and over again the same phrase 'I shall cast them forth with silence' and that Fitch called out after him but the Reverend didn't take notice. Fitch said he didn't think anything of it until he heard of what had happened to the child and the Reverend's wife. He said he went to the sheriff to report because he felt uneasy with what he heard and saw that day."

"October 20th, 1836. I stopped to take tea with Sally Paul Demers. She was not well, and was alone with her thoughts of her daughter, Polly, and her grand-daughter, Silence. She had her Bible out and we prayed together. The District Attorney came to question Sally Paul, she told them the Reverend Winters was a disagreeable man, often mad as a march hare, and he became more so after the birth of his only child Silence. I was distressed and made no attempts to direct her as she spoke. After the District Attorney left, I prayed with her for the souls of Polly and Silence. Sally's words, "I shall see them no more, but they will remain," brought chills to my bones. I had a miserable day and night of

it. My mind is wandering of thoughts of what happened at that pond. In my heart, I fear the worse."

"Thursday, November 3rd, 1836. I decided to go to the meeting house to attend the court, this trial has consumed the whole town of Eden. The trial has divided us, those who believe the Reverend is of guilt, and those who believe his innocence. A number of the town men are calling for an investigation of the death of Louisa Ann Putnam and believe the Reverend Winters was to blame. I actually heard men outside the meeting house yelling, 'Hang him! Hang him! for he is guilty.' "

"November 10th, 1836. States Attorney Herschel Chandler came calling to talk with Polly Winters' mother, Sally Paul Demers. He broke the news that the Reverend Winters was discharged as they could not bring sufficient evidence to prove his guilt in the drownings of his wife and daughter. Sally Paul fainted upon hearing the news. This evening, my brother Henry came home, shaken, after having witnessed Reverend Winters being dragged by his horse, Henry said he fears the Reverend will not survive his injuries. Henry described being on the road in front of the Reverend's house, hearing a scream right before he saw the horse rear up, throwing the Reverend. Henry explained he believes the horse was spooked by the scream. Henry continued to say the Reverend's foot was caught and he estimated the Reverend was dragged at least 30 feet, body and head hitting many rocks and downed trees. Henry did his best to make the Reverend comfortable before going to fetch the doctor. He said the screaming and the blood from the Reverend is an image he will never let rest."

"November 11th, 1836. My brothers Henry and

Tom said the Reverend is not expected to survive the night. Some of the people in town who believed the Reverend killed his wife and daughter are celebrating the news of the Reverend's demise at the tavern. Henry and Tom said our brother Fitch joined the men at the tavern to celebrate what they termed "the dying evil Reverend." A group formed at the old Meeting House to pray for him. I will continue to pray for healing for this town."

"November 14th, 1836. Fitch came home with news the Reverend Winters has died. Fitch told a story of one of the nurses caring for the Reverend described that his skin had turned to a waxen pallor, his breathing was shallow, and she knew that he had not long in this world. I will pray for his soul but know in my heart that he harmed his wife and daughter. My brother Fitch talked of the Reverend's death being justice for the harm that he inflicted on his wife Polly and young daughter Silence. He believes that the Reverend also harmed Louisa Putnam. I joined Fitch in this belief. My prayers to God are to heal this town and to ease the troubling thoughts in my own head and heart. God have mercy on all of our souls."

Chapter 26

He woke to the sound of thunder echoing off the mountains and then heard her cries. Jack felt her body next to his, thrashing, tied up in the sheets. The dream held her under, and he had difficulty waking her out of it. He pulled her closer to him and pressed a light kiss to her forehead.

"You're okay, you're okay, just a dream. I'm right here," he murmured in her ear.

"I was dreaming of the Reverend but then his face..."

"What? Who were you dreaming about?"

"I was having a nightmare, it was horrible."

Jack heard the despair in her voice, ran his hands down her back, as she took three deep breaths. She moved to curl her body closer around his and pressed her face close to his chest.

"Do you want to tell me about it?"

"Yes, but I want to record it so I don't forget any of the details. I need my phone." She sat upright and scanned the room for her phone.

"You record them to...?

"To remember, it helps."

"Where is it, Rebecca? I'll get it." Jack rose from the bed.

"Over by the dresser, charging."

He located the phone, handed it to her. As she set

the phone to record, he climbed in next to her and wrapped her in his arms. "I was dreaming about the man who built this house, Reverend Winters. It was after a wedding, his wedding, he and his wife, Polly." Her voice hitched as she continued. "In the dream, Polly and Reverend Winters are walking, hand and hand, down the path behind the house to the pond. Polly is happy. I see her face, she's happy with her husband, she's smiling, looking up at him. Polly's proud to have such an important man. She's wearing a wedding dress, it's white satin, it's beautiful. Pink flowers dot her hair. I'm walking behind them on the path, watching as they move toward the pond. They get to the pond, and he drops her hand, his eyes are hard and dark, menacing.

"Jack, there is something wrong with the Reverend, the way he is looking changed when they reach the pond. It's awful, he starts to call her horrible names. She's confused, she doesn't understand what's happening. She calls him by his first name, Hiram, his first name is Hiram. He yells at her to call him Reverend, only Reverend. He demands she take off her dress. She doesn't understand what's happening. She's scared. She doesn't want to take off her dress. He yells at her to take it off. He takes off his belt. Jack, she's so scared. I can see her shaking, her whole body is trembling with fear and…" Rebecca paused.

"Do you want to stop?"

"No, I need to get it out. I need to finish it."

"Okay."

Rebecca took a deep breath and continued. "I can feel her confusion, she's frightened, she doesn't understand what's happening. She knows something is terribly wrong with him. He looks possessed. I hear him in my head, he's telling her, 'Whores don't wear white, take it off.' She's embarrassed, shocked to be called a whore. She tries to reason with him. She's young and inexperienced. She's never been with a man. He keeps insisting, his anger growing, telling her to take off the dress. He keeps saying he needs to teach her how to be an obedient wife. Obedience is God's path to being a good wife. He tells her he needs to beat the whore out of her if she's to be a good wife, it's God's way. He forces her to remove her clothing, has her put her hands on the tree, the big maple tree next to the pond. You know the tree out back?"

"I do know the tree, it's a beautiful old tree."

"Jack, she's naked, she can't see him, but can hear him. He's behind her," she said, struggling.

"Take your time, Rebecca."

"I can feel how scared she is, she can hear him, hear the belt, he's behind her, she's facing the pond. She's so scared Jack, he's whipping her with his belt. She's begging and pleading which only encourages him, arouses him. Jack, it's awful, I could feel her pain, her confusion, and how scared she was. He raped her. He raped his wife," she said before she collapsed into his arms and held him tight.

Chapter 27

When Jack woke the next morning, he smelled the bacon cooking. He lay in bed, thinking about the night, Rebecca's nightmare, and her reaction. *What the hell was that all about?* Concerned, he stretched. His dog Keeper raised his head from the dog bed on the floor, scampered over to Jack's bedside, tail wagging, and placed his head next to Jack's hand. "Hey there, boy, you ready to get up?" Keeper nudged Jack's hand with his nose. "Yep, I smell it too, Keep, definitely bacon. It sure smells good." After giving Keeper a thorough scratch behind the ears, Jack rose out of bed and pulled on his worn Eden Volunteer Fire Department T-shirt over his boxers. Following the smell of bacon, he made his way to the kitchen with Keep on his heels.

He slipped into the kitchen and found her over the stove, hair tied back in a loose ponytail. Bacon sizzled in a pan, fresh oranges had been cut for juicing, and what appeared to be quiche and a loaf of bread were baking in the oven. She turned, saw him in the doorway, and smiled.

"Hey, sleepyhead," she said, closing the oven door.

"Hey, yourself." He crossed the room and wrapped his arms around her.

"You still feel nice and warm," she said burrowing her body into his. "How'd you sleep?"

"Truthfully, not great, it was hard to fall back to

sleep after hearing about your nightmare."

"I'm sorry about that."

"No need to be sorry. How long have you been up? Looks like you've made enough food to feed an army," Jack said as he stepped back and glanced down at her. He noticed the dark shadows under her eyes and ran a finger over one. He studied her face.

"I know, I've had better nights."

"How often do you get them?"

"The dreams?" Rebecca turned toward the oven and answered. "Lately, more often than I want to admit. They're increasing for sure. Reading the diaries yesterday got to me. The dreams are adding another layer to the story. The energy in the house is potent, almost physical. It's hard to explain. I have a feeling there's a story that needs to be told. I feel it in my bones. Cooking is good therapy—it helps ease the worry."

"Are you sure that's all? Just the research, reading the diaries, or is there something else going on?"

"There is something...I know this sounds crazy, but I can't seem to shake the feeling that..." She swallowed hard.

"What? What feeling?"

"That I'm being watched. Maybe I'm losing my mind, or maybe I'm not as settled in this old house as I think I am." She gave a little laugh but wouldn't meet his eyes. The beeper on the coffee sounded.

He went to the coffeemaker, poured two generous cups, and set the large cup in front of her. "Okay, now, tell me more about this feeling of being watched."

"I'm not sure how to explain the feeling. It comes over me. I'll be doing ordinary things, hanging laundry, walking the dogs, making dinner, and the feeling washes over me. Almost like a presence, sometimes it's a quiet knowing, something's there, in the shadows, watching and waiting. At times, it feels threatening, and other times comforting. I don't know. It's hard to explain."

"Rebecca, I want you to be honest with me."

She tilted her head. "Okay?"

"I get the feeling there's more to this story that you aren't sharing." He placed his hand on top of hers. "At some point, you're going to need to trust me."

She looked down at her hands. "You're right. I do have more to tell you."

Rebecca didn't want to keep the truth of who she was from him. It took her years to come to terms with who and what she became after the botched abduction. She needed to trust him. Worst-case scenario he'd kick her to the curb, but in her heart, she didn't believe Jack was that kind of guy. "Jack, how about we eat first, and then take a long walk? I need food," she said wearily. "I promise after we eat, I will tell you everything."

Rising, she moved to the oven to remove the quiche. All three dogs glued themselves to her, just waiting for a piece of quiche to hit the floor. Jack laughed at the three dogs' eager faces. "Do you see this?" he said trying to lighten the mood.

"Looks like I have a house full of men who want to be fed, and all have an affinity for bacon." Rebecca turned to the pups. "Guys, maybe we'll save you some."

"It's not looking good, guys." He laughed, shoving a piece of bacon in his mouth.

Chapter 28

The midday light embraced them as they walked in the field. Jack followed the sun's path as it danced upon Rebecca's face making her freckles pop. She took his breath away. As they turned to hike back to the house with the dogs, Jack reached for her hand, to hold in his. Her hair fell loose down her back in soft raven sun-kissed curls, her cheeks rosy with heat. Jack thought his heart might stop and prayed to the universe that he could spend the rest of his days soaking in her beauty.

He stopped to hold her to him, his hands caressing her. She reached up, nuzzled and kissed his neck. She drove him crazy. God, he was falling and falling hard. He knew he found her, the one. The overwhelming desire he felt for Rebecca was nothing he'd ever experienced with another woman. This time he took control, he shifted her body away from him, leaned her back against him, granting him full access. He slowly unbuttoned her shirt, his hands embracing each one of her breasts. Letting his thumbs travel over each of her nipples, willing them to attention. He moved her hair to one side giving his lips access to her neck. He fixed his mouth to nip and taste and caught the aroma of citrus from her soap.

With his hands caressing and his mouth nipping, her moans deepened—giving him permission to take what he wanted. He let his hand drop to the top button on her pants, slipped a hand under the lace she wore, found her wet and hot with need.

"Jack, oh God!" she cried as he worked his fingers on her. She arched her body forward against his hand with each movement, her breaths coming out in short gasps. He continued kneading the soft swollen spot, filled with need. Her head fell back on his shoulder as he used his fingers to guide her body closer to the edge. He felt the orgasm building, knowing she was lost in the pleasure, and took her to the point of no return. Jack held her tight as she cried out, and felt her body ride out the last waves of the orgasm against him. He trailed his fingertips up her arms, felt the goosebumps form, and heard one more moan escape between her lips. She turned and rose up on her toes to gently kiss him, wrapped her arms around him, and laid her head on his chest.

She took his hand and walked him over to the large rock overlooking the field. He sat and studied her, in awe of her beauty as she shimmied the rest of her jeans down her legs. At that moment, watching her, he thanked the universe for letting her into his life. She came to him, bent her head down, nipped his lower lip between her teeth before she plunged her mouth over his. He guided her body, so she straddled him, allowing him full access to her soft depths. The tightness of her enflamed his urgency, his thrusts growing in intensity, faster, over and over until together they cried out. They held on to each other, limp and weak, trying to recover.

"You're amazing," was all he said, his breath hot against her ear. He felt her arms link around his frame tighter than before, felt her racing heart. *Yup,* he thought to himself, *she's full of surprises.*

As he sat on the rock and pulled on his jeans, she lowered her head for one last kiss. He helped to button the rest of her shirt before she joined him back on the rock.

"Rebecca, I think Manny's pissed. Look at the way he's staring at me."

"He sees you as competition. He's a smart boy."

With his head hung low, Manny waited for Rebecca's command. She patted his head and gave him the sign to lie down. He moved to her feet, pawed at the grass, circled three times, and lay down and sulked.

"He's very protective of you." Jack smiled, looking at all three dogs around them, and thought—*what a great canine family.*

"He is very loyal. I count on them as much as they count on me. For a long time, Max and Manny were all I had."

"I'm glad you have them. Especially living out here all alone in the country."

"Jack, I know we got a bit sidetracked."

"You can sidetrack me anytime you want." He touched his lips to the back of her hand.

She kissed him back. "My heart and head are telling me to trust you with the truth. Like I said before, you're right, I haven't shared the whole story with you," she began.

"Anytime you want to start, Rebecca, I'm right here. I've been told I'm an excellent listener."

"I've been holding back. I guess some habits are hard to break. I suppose I'm afraid of what you'll think of me, or how it might change the way you see me."

He reached again for her hand. "Rebecca, it's been my experience fearing the response is usually worse than the actual response. Just tell me."

"I will, but I need to ask you, if you would, just first hear me out first, with no judgment. Okay?"

He placed their hands on her leg, in hopes of calming her nerves.

"It's going to be okay. Just tell me." His voice was soft and reassuring. "Come on, what is it?"

Nervous, she took a big breath and began. "When you had your accident, when the branch hurt your leg. I felt it. I knew."

"Well, of course, you did, you found me."

"No, you don't see. I knew because I sensed it. I sensed someone was hurt when I was standing in the kitchen. It hit me."

"What do you mean? Like a gut feeling?"

"Kind of, maybe it would help if I start at the beginning."

"Okay."

"When I was seven, I went through a traumatic experience. A man tried to abduct me. I was with my brothers at a playground and became separated from them. I ended up badly hurt. I don't know if you remember the story, it was in the newspapers and on TV in the late 90s. The abductions happened in Boston—there were a string of young children abducted. Some even killed. I was one of the lucky ones. I survived."

Jack folded his arms in front of his body and stared down at the ground. Hearing her words and the realization that someone hurt her hit him in the gut. He let out a deep sigh. "I do remember the story…it was all over the news. It scared the shit out of me, and to, now, know that you…" He took a ragged inhale and paced.

"I know it's hard to hear, Jack, but please just listen. It happened a *long* time ago. I am fine now. Look at me. I'm fine. I survived. Look at me."

He paused, peered into her green eyes, saw the strong and brave woman he loved, and thanked God for her. "Okay."

"When this man tried to abduct me, I ended up falling from a moving car. I had significant injuries from the fall. Injuries requiring a medically induced coma to heal. I woke up from the accident different."

"Different? How?" He asked.

"I was never the same after I woke up. I was no longer a carefree seven-year-old kid. She was gone. I realized after that day the world wasn't a safe place, even when you had a loving and caring family. Bad things can still happen. I have worked through a lot of the trauma, but a part of it has stayed with me. It profoundly changed me. And, for some reason I can't explain, it ties me to other people."

He narrowed his eyes at her. "What do you mean, other people? Do you mean the other children who were hurt?"

"Yes, but also to people who are hurting physically or emotionally or both."

"I remember reading they caught the guy because one girl survived. That was you?"

"It was. Actually, two of us survived. After I woke up, thanks to a police officer who listened and believed in me, I identified the girl who was abducted after me. I sensed her pain. I knew where she was. I knew what she wore. I knew the address where he was holding her. Even the color of the building."

"What? How is that possible? What do you mean

you knew the address? You 'identified' her?"

"It's hard to explain the unexplainable. The process of how I receive information is hard to put into words. Truthfully, the knowing comes over me. It's kinda like knowing the phone's going to ring before it rings."

"How did your doctors explain it?"

"They speculate parts of my brain, possibly in the limbic system, that focus on emotion and memory were altered somehow from the accident. Or maybe altered as a result of the coma, or a combination of the two. My doctors had no definitive answers for me on why I woke with this heightened ability to read people."

"What actually happens? Can you describe it?"

"Each time it happens, it's unique to the person or situation. I can't begin to tell you how frustrating it is. To not understand why some people's thoughts come to me, or why I feel what they're feeling or experiencing. Or how I know their life story without knowing them."

"So the information just comes to you?"

"Yes, it's similar to having the experience of knowing what a person is going to say before they say it? Has that ever happened to you?"

"Sure, it happens all the time with my dad."

"Well, this is like that, but multiplied by a thousand. It's like my intuition is in overdrive. When it comes on strong, the images, the knowing hits me like a tidal wave. It knocks the breath right out of me. Sometimes I see a couple of images, other times I see the whole picture like a movie playing in my head. That's what happened with Murphy, the police officer who sat with me in my hospital room when I was seven. I described all of the scenes like I was watching a movie. The police were able to capture the perpetrator and free Allison, the girl, he was holding after my talk with Murphy. And the other thing is…the person I'm receiving information from doesn't have to be alive."

"You mean like in, in…?" He stopped.

"Yes, Jack, people who have passed away. It's not frightening, just, sometimes, exhausting and overwhelming. The first time I realized I was reading someone who'd passed away was when I was nine. My grandmother, who died when I was six, came to me and told me to go to my mother and tell her…" Rebecca paused.

"Tell her what, Rebecca?"

"She wanted me to tell my mother she loved her and was always proud of her."

"That had to freak you out some."

"Actually, it made me happy. Still does today to think of that time. I was happy to see my Grandma again and so proud she chose me to deliver such an important message to my mom."

"How'd your mother react?"

"Initially she looked at me like I had two heads. It freaked her out. And then she asked how I knew at that exact moment she was thinking about whether or not her mother was ever proud of her."

"And you answered her thoughts."

"I did. I knew. I did what my grandma told me to do."

He raked a hand down his face before sitting back down next to her and took hold of her hand.

"And the nightmares?" he asked.

"Yes, the nightmares are not particularly pleasant. I think each one of the dreams is a piece of the puzzle, giving me more information about the history of the house and its previous owners. I guess I should be careful what I wish for."

"What do you mean? Careful what you wish for?"

"I think my desire to understand the history of the house has unearthed a lot of secrets. Cam Winters is often in my dreams. I think buying this house has somehow psychically tied me to him. His ancestors built the house. He's tied to this as much as I am, maybe more. Don't get me wrong. I want to know what happened, but it does weigh on me, not just the dreams and the sleep deprivation, but the aftermath."

He looked at her and saw the toll, the dark circles.

"Truthfully, I'm not sure I know what to say or how to respond to all this. It's not something you hear every day."

"It's part of who I am." She read it in his eyes as they fell to the ground, turning away from hers as he sat silent. "If you can't deal with it, tell me now," she exploded, her green eyes engulfed with heat. "When I look into your eyes it's like looking at an accumulation of people over the years who stared at me like I was a freak. I expected more from you."

Jack stared at the ground, giving him time to pause, and then he heard her tears. "Rebecca, I need a minute. Okay? You have been living with this since the age of seven. I'm just trying to process right now what you're telling me. Please don't cry." He watched her body tighten.

"God damn it, can you just give me a minute? I don't know how to feel about all of this! Jesus. Just give me a minute to fucking process all of it," he shouted, matching her temper.

"Well, process faster," she countered, wiping the

tears. She exhaled loudly and turned to face him. "Jack, you need to understand, sometimes I hate that I'm different. I just want to be normal. I didn't ask for this, to feel other people's emotions, thoughts, to be bombarded. Sometimes my own feelings are way too much for me, especially now, especially with us."

Jack held out his hand, his eyes meeting hers. When he felt the warmth of her hand in his, he pulled her in tight to comfort and hold. "I can't even imagine what you go through. I'm having a hard time wrapping my head around it, but I'm sorry for your burden."

"But?" she said quietly.

"But from my heart, I love who you are, and for the record, I love where we are headed." Jack brought her hand up to his lips and kissed it tenderly.

"Me too, Jack, me too." She laid her head back against him and let more tears spill.

He took his hand and gently wiped away the tears from her cheeks and pulled her to him even closer. He linked his hand with hers to hold and wondered to himself where the hell they'd go from here.

Chapter 29

Crescent House Inn was a large Victorian beauty that sat magnificently on top of a hill on Main Street. The house served as the locus for the town, commanding respect from all the residents scattered below. A beautiful, rounded, wrap-around porch with ornamental spindles and brackets seduced visitors to sit in rocking chairs and socialize. The Victorian was endowed with wings and bays in many directions, which only added to the feel of grandeur. Today the house was decorated with loads of mums, greenery, and patriotic flags on all the porches in honor of the day— the perfect spot to watch the Labor Day Parade as it made its way down Main Street.

As Jack and Rebecca approached the stairs leading to the grand house, she felt her chest constrict, stopped in her tracks, and grabbed his hand.

"Jack, you do know the whole town is talking about us?"

Jack, seeing Rebecca's horror, burst into laughter and placed her hand on his heart.

"I've heard a thing or two. Eden's a small town. Think of it this way, we're providing some good comic relief for the town. Personally, I think small-town gossip provides a good community service."

"What do you mean?"

"Well, the way I figure, this town is filled with

hardworking people, people raising families, worried about paying bills and putting food on the table. You and I, we're a bit of a distraction or better yet, entertainment from the worry and boredom of the everyday grind. Let's give them something to talk about."

She laughed as he sang and pulled his face to hers for a kiss.

Behind Jack's shoulder, Rebecca spotted the older couple, slowly, gingerly make their way toward them. She tapped Jack who turned and waved at the old couple, with what looked like years and years of history etched across their faces. Rebecca noticed the man held the woman's hand before raising it to his lips for a quick kiss, and how the woman, in return, tenderly patted the man's cheek. The old couple stopped in front of them and smiled.

"Mary, Glenn, how are you? Rebecca, this is the Parkers, from whom you bought the house."

Rebecca noticed the sweetness in the couple's eyes as they looked up at her.

"Jack," Mary said as she reached past her husband to give Jack a big hug.

"Rebecca, nice to finally meet you. I know you dealt with our oldest son, Cole, during the closing. He spoke so highly of you. It makes us feel so good to know our house is in loving hands." Glenn said.

"Cole was wonderful, so helpful, and he left me with a bunch of detailed notes about the house. I really appreciated his help."

"We're glad to hear. The decision to sell our house was difficult. We loved that old cape. How are you liking it?" Mary inquired.

"I love it, although, I would love to pick your brain about all the noises."

Glenn leaned in. "It's an old house, makes a lot of sounds. The banging sound from the pipes in the winter can be alarming if you're not used to it."

"I'll remember that. I know this might sound a bit odd, but did you ever hear, maybe, a child's voice? Giggling?" she asked.

"No, I can't say we ever did, but we'd often joke that a child was playing tricks on us—just small things like keys being moved, the channel on the TV switching automatically to a children's channel when we would be watching the news. We'd laugh, and I'd say to Mary, 'Hannah is up to her old tricks.' We named our little ghost. It was all harmless, she wasn't malicious, just enjoyed practical jokes now and then," Glenn said as he smiled down at his wife.

"As soon as we talked to her, she would quiet down. We liked having our little ghost. In truth, the nest didn't feel quite as empty having her around," Mary said as Glenn rubbed her back tenderly.

"I'm curious, how come you thought your ghost was a girl?" Rebecca asked, sensing Mary's strong intuition.

"You know I never thought of it. I guess I just had a feeling."

"I know exactly what you mean. It was great meeting you both. Anytime you want to come out and visit, the door is always open."

"Thank you, dear, I would love to see what you've done with the place." Mary patted Rebecca's hand.

"We should all probably get in before the food's gone," Glenn said, ushering his wife along.

"Well, we wouldn't want Glenn here to miss out. He's always thinking about food."

Jack and Rebecca laughed as the Parkers, hand in hand, climbed the steps to the party.

"Sweet couple," Rebecca said.

"They really are, married forever, they just fit," Jack said.

"They do." Rebecca pointed up to the Victorian house. "Are we ready to give them something to talk about?"

"Why don't we start here," he said, circling his arms about her.

"Come on! You heard Glenn; we wouldn't want to miss the food."

"Okay, but for the record, I would be fine missing the food."

"Come on, you." Rebecca escorted Jack toward the stairs, who in turn gave her butt a gentle squeeze as they headed up the stairs to the large wooden ornamental front door. The sound of music and conversation filled the air. People sat scattered on the front porch in groups, some leaning against the porch rail, drinking beer and laughing.

"Ready?" he asked.

"Ready," she said.

As Jack opened the large wooden door, a shock went through her. She noticed all eyes were on them, and with a deep breath, she stepped into the room. The choppy wave of people's thoughts nearly knocked her over, and she grabbed at Jack's hand to steady herself. *Be grateful all these people are not crammed into your house.* And with another exhale and years of practice, she controlled the volume of noise in her head and worked up the courage to mingle. She considered a trip to the bathroom, locking herself in for a few minutes to breathe.

The large living area held what seemed to be a hundred people crammed in every corner and crevice. Soft jazz played in the background, while laughter and the hum of conversation filled the room. The scent of summer barbecue hit her; barbecued ribs had her mouth watering and her stomach rumbling with anticipation. At first glance, Rebecca didn't recognize a soul. She looked around the room as the anxiety rushed her. She regretted not taking a couple of minutes of quiet behind a locked door to sort through the wave of people's thoughts and emotions that struck her, knowing it would help her get her bearings. Her eyes landed on Tom Attwell, a familiar face making his way toward her with a tray full of drinks. She immediately felt her heart rate slow seeing Tom's kind face and feeling Jack's arm around her waist.

"Jack," Peter Covington yelled over the crowd, as he and his partner Tom walked up.

"Peter, Tom, the house looks great. Tom, I know you and Rebecca met at the library. Peter, this is Rebecca," Jack said.

Rebecca stared at the man walking with Tom, his deep brown eyes and wavy brown hair. He could've been Jack's twin except for the scar that ran along his jawline and the small diamond stud earring he wore in his right ear.

"Rebecca, a real pleasure to meet you." Peter leaned over to give Rebecca a quick kiss on the cheek. "It's nice to see a smile on my friend's face again. I'm guessing you had something to do with that." Peter held out the tray of drinks out to Jack. Jack grabbed a glass of champagne for Rebecca and a beer for himself.

"Your house is gorgeous. I'd love a tour, if you two can find a spare minute," Rebecca said.

"Oh, Jack can show you the house. God, he probably knows more about it than the two of us. Corcoran and Sons essentially put this beauty back in shape," Tom mused.

"Food is in the dining room. Have a good time, and hopefully, we can catch up later. Tom and I have to make our way to the porch and serve drinks before our guests revolt." Peter and Tom zigged and zagged through the crowded living room. Both stopped to greet guests on the way. Loud clapping and laughter erupted as they finally reached the porch.

"Rebecca, hi." Carol waved as she called out, navigating through the crowd with a drink in hand. Rebecca noticed Carol's blonde hair, usually in a tight bun, was down, outlining her shoulders in soft curls. She wore a snug peacock blue dress that made her blue eyes pop, and she teetered on gold sandals, adding at least three inches to her frame.

"Carol," Rebecca said, relieved to see a familiar face. "You look stunning—very sexy!"

"Thank you, I really tried. It feels good."

"Very nice, indeed," Jack said.

"Well, thank you, Jack. Do you mind if I steal Rebecca for a minute?"

"Of course. I'm going to go snag some of those spinach pie thingies and find the damn ribs I'm smelling."

"Jack, do you mind snagging me a plate? I'm starving."

"You got it, Hon." Rebecca smiled at the term of endearment he used as he left.

"You two are adorable, and speaking of adorable, oh my," Carol said.

Rebecca followed Carol's eyes that landed straight on Camden Winters, who stood alone. Rebecca gave her a *What the fuck are you thinking?* eye roll.

"I know! I know exactly what you're thinking, but look, I'd really like someone who isn't attached to notice my skintight dress and come hither heels. Cam's got quite the reputation, but part of me thinks he's just misunderstood."

"Really? Well, okay, maybe, but we do know some of his family's history, and you know the old adage, the apple doesn't fall far from the tree. And, in Cam's case, I think it's true."

"Maybe you're right, but who and what you come from doesn't have to define you."

"You're a truly good person." Rebecca raised her glass to Carol in a toast and sipped.

"Yeah, I'm not sure my intention are all that honorable. I'm a woman in lust. And that man is hot. He exudes...I don't know...some sort of male pheromones on steroids. I swear, my ovaries are jumping with joy just looking at him. They are literally screaming 'let's make a baby.' I have lost all control."

"You better find some and fast. He's trouble with a capital T."

"But...just look at the way he moves, God, it puts all sorts of ideas in my head, and those bedroom eyes," Carol said.

"I'll give him that—his eyes are stunning."

"Oh my, Rebecca, watch how Cam's lips caress the

canapé, like he's making love to it. I'd like to switch places with that."

"Please stop, I don't want to have to call 911 again," Rebecca joked. "We both know, he knows he's hot, and, in my book, that's one huge turn-off. Plus my mother, who is a very wise woman, once told me never trust a man with bedroom eyes. And Camden Winters is unpredictable, and not in a good way."

"True, but, maybe, I could get lost in those bedroom eyes for just one night? What's the harm?"

"What's the harm in a meaningless hook-up? Please tell me you're kidding. Should I give you the complete list or just partial of why it's a bad idea?"

"Okay, I'm kidding, sort of, but living in a small town blows when you want to date. I know everyone at this party. Anyway, switching gears, the research, any thoughts about Hattie's diary?" Carol asked, sipping on her champagne.

"It's certainly hard not to jump to conclusions."

"Agreed. I've been thinking about requesting the archives on the District Attorney's notes on the investigation of Reverend Winters. The questions about him, his family, Polly, and Silence keep piling up for me. I have a lot of theories floating around my head."

"I do as well. What are you thinking?" Rebecca asked.

"Well, we have a witness, Hattie's brother Fitch, who saw Reverend Winters walking away from the pond instead of walking toward it. Also, why wouldn't the Reverend be calling out for help? And Hattie writes her brother mentioned hearing what sounded like a bobcat."

"How is that relevant?" Rebecca asked.

"Bobcats are known to shriek like a woman in pain, or a woman being attacked. It's a terrifying noise to hear. One time, I actually called the State Police, convinced a woman was being attacked in the woods behind my house. Typically you only hear a bobcat at night and only if you live in a very rural, isolated location where bobcats roam."

"So, you think what Fitch heard was not a bobcat but Polly Winters?"

"Exactly."

"I can imagine if you witness your child being harmed, or your child drowning, that could cause a mother to go into hysterics."

"That type of pain and shrieking could very well mimic the sound of a bobcat," Carol mused.

"The thought of it makes the hairs on my arm stand up."

"And what about what Hattie wrote about what her brother Fitch heard the Reverend saying as he walked down the path. 'I shall cast them forth with silence.' My gut is telling me he did exactly that—he silenced his wife and child by drowning them."

Rebecca sipped her drink and mulled over Carol's words. She knew she needed to confide in Carol about her dreams, and the encounters with spirits at home. Her eyes met Carol's.

"Carol, I've been having a lot of disturbing dreams, actually nightmares about Polly and the Reverend at the pond. I think in some way my dreams are providing me a window to seeing the truth."

"Well, if you believe that dreams pick up on energy, then I think your theory about your dreams is accurate. I get the feeling we've stumbled upon the ultimate cold case. I'm loving the mystery of what we're uncovering, but it's so hard to absorb the sadness of it."

"I wish I could say I'm enjoying the mystery. We've opened up pandora's box, and part of me wishes we never had. I'm afraid what lies in the box possesses more energy than can be contained."

"You're right, much like your dreams. I don't think trying to contain it is going to work."

"At the moment, living in my house is anything but peaceful. There's a strong presence there, and it wants my attention."

"Like a haunting?"

"Maybe Polly and Silence need us to help right a wrong. Hattie's diaries hint that all is not well between the couple and cast doubts on the Reverend's character. She knew something was amiss in Polly's house. Hattie knew something was amiss with the Reverend. My dreams support her writings," Rebecca contemplated.

"How do we help Polly and Silence find peace?"

"I wish I had the answer to that question."

Chapter 30

Cam Winters, drink in hand, made his way across the room, his eyes on the prize. A sly smile formed as he checked out Carol. *Seriously,* he thought to himself, *great bod on this broad.* Cam wondered to himself what they would think of a three-way, smiled at the image of watching Carol and Rebecca kissing, with Carol's hands on Rebecca's full breasts, and then, slowly they'd turn all their attention to him. A bump from behind had Cam cursing, having spilled half his beer on his new khakis and jolting him out of his fantasy.

Carol and Rebecca looked up to find Cam dabbing at his pants with a paper napkin.

"Rebecca, Carol, enjoying the party?"

Jack weaved his way through the crowd. He gave Cam a cool stare as he, not so subtly, wrapped an arm around Rebecca. "What do you want, Cam?"

"Just came over to say hello to the ladies, Jack. Nice to see you too."

"Well, now, you can say goodbye."

Carol tapped Rebecca on the arm. "I think I'm gonna go and get another drink before someone throws a punch," she whispered.

"That sounds like a good idea. I'll catch up with you later."

Rebecca placed a hand to Jack's face, turned him toward her, and in front of Cam and the whole party kissed him. "I love you, Jack Corcoran."

"I love you too, Rebecca McCabe," he said, cupping her face and covering her lips with his.

"Woah! Get a room, you two. Upstairs to the left," Peter said as he strolled by with a tray full of drinks.

The crowd erupted with laughter and cheers.

****

Maureen Corcoran watched her brother and Rebecca from across the room with her sister Kathleen by her side. With a searing look that could kill, Maureen leaned over to her sister and whispered, "Our brother's in trouble, mark my words, Rebecca is a total stage-five-clinger."

"He looks pretty happy to me, Maureen. If anything, they're both stage five, which I think is pretty sweet. It's nice to see our brother in love," Kathleen pointed out.

"Time will tell. I'm still on the fence about her. There's just something I don't like."

"Stop it." Kathleen nudged her sister with her elbow. "Give her a chance. You're way too protective of Jack. If you haven't noticed, he's a grown man who can make his own decisions."

"I know, I just don't think I can stand seeing our baby brother hurt again. And like most men, they think with their dicks first. We both know Jack has a huge heart.

"I'm glad you said heart."

"Funny, Kathleen, very funny,"

"Anyway, Maureen, who said she's going to hurt him? We don't know. All I'm saying is give her a chance, get to know her, and *try to be nice!*" Kathleen said, as she gently pushed her sister in Rebecca's direction.

Give her a chance. Why should I? she thought as she stepped between the party guests. Maureen found Rebecca over by the table filled with hors d'oeuvres. Maureen smirked. *Sweetheart, your figure doesn't need any of those, a moment on the lips forever on the hips.* She stifled a laugh. *Cattiness is so underrated.*

"So, you love my brother?" Maureen said, with an uber-bitch voice.

"I do, in fact, love your brother. Is there a problem?"

"I don't know, you tell me. Don't you think it's all happening a bit too fast?"

"Yes, it is, and I think it does when you find the right one." Rebecca shrugged her shoulders.

"So, you think my brother is the right one?"

"Yes, he is, at least, for me. Whatever problem you have with me, Maureen, doesn't change the fact, like it or not, I love your brother."

"Okay," Maureen said, not cracking a smile.

"That's it, just okay?" Rebecca stood stunned.

"Yeah, okay, just don't hurt him," Maureen responded, her blue eyes hardened.

"I don't plan on hurting him."

"Jack's been hurt in the past. In fact, the woman who hurt him reminds me of you. I'm just not sure I trust you when it comes to my baby brother."

"You don't even know me. And, for the record, I'm not sure I trust you either. Truth, Maureen, you come across as a mixture of a bitch and a bully. Not traits I want in a friend."

"Well, I guess it's good we're not looking to be friends." Maureen sneered as she grabbed a glass of wine. "Also, you might want to lay off the stuffed mushrooms, a moment on the lips," she said, as she walked away.

"Bitch," Rebecca said under her breath.

Maureen stood in the archway and rolled her eyes as she watched her brother Jack with Rebecca. She knew her brother was a hopeless romantic and, someday, would need his big sister when this current woman broke his heart.

"Hey, Maureen, get back over here," Jack summoned.

Reluctantly, Maureen crossed the room to them. "Problem with the leg?"

"No, the leg is fine. I'm just wondering if you and Rebecca arranged a time to go to the gym yet?"

"No, we haven't yet." Maureen gave her brother a half smile while she crossed her arms in front of her defensively.

"No time like the present."

Maureen felt the not-so-subtle nudge from her brother's elbow in her side.

"Rebecca, how about Thursday morning? I teach a wall ball class called, 'Balls to the Wall,' starts at five?" *Please say no.* Maureen all but willed it as she looked at Rebecca's face.

"I think I can make that work."

Fuck. "Okay, I'll see you there, Covington Crossfit on State."

"Right, looking forward to it." *Not.*

"I'm glad you two finally found some time to spend with each other. Rebecca, we should probably get going though? I'm sure the dogs would welcome a walk before it gets too late."

"Sounds good to me. Let me just go and say goodbye to Carol," Rebecca said, leaving Jack and Maureen alone.

"I'm glad you like her," Jack said, turning to his sister.

"She's a peach," Maureen said, behind clenched teeth.

"She really is."

****

From across the room, Maureen's twin sister Kathleen, her new baby in her arms, saw the look of contempt on her twin's face. Rocking her new baby in her arms, she zigzagged across the room to offer support and, maybe, some words of wisdom. "Now that wasn't so bad, was it?" Kathleen said as she patted her baby's butt, doing the mama hip dance.

Maureen rolled her eyes. "Jury's out, I'll see if I can make her puke during the workout. Let's just see how tough she really is."

"Come on, Maureen, just give her a chance. Jack looks happier than I've ever seen him."

"Yeah, but will it stick?"

Kathleen shook her head in disgust and pointed a finger at her sister. "Now that's just plain mean, and you know it. Jack deserves to be happy. Give Rebecca a chance."

"Why should I?"

"Maybe, because she puts a smile on our brother's face. Have you ever stopped to consider it might be time to give up the mean girl routine? Could be one of the reasons you're still single."

"Jesus, Kathleen, a bit below the belt! Don't you think? If you weren't holding the cutest baby in the world, I'd kick your ass right now."

"All I'm saying is it might be a good time to do a little internal inventory. I, for one, am glad Jack's happy. I'd like to be able to say the same about you someday," Kathleen said, feeling her husband Greg's arms around her.

"Who's happy?" Greg asked.

"Jack is. So am I, by the way." Kathleen grinned and kissed her husband's cheek.

"Me too, Mama! You ready to roll? Or do you want me to find a quiet room so you can breastfeed this little munchkin?"

"You two look like you need some serious sleep," Maureen observed.

"Part of being parents to a newborn. I'm *so* ready for quiet, and to be rocking this little one at home. Greg, can you gather the rest of the kids?" Kathleen leaned in to give Maureen a hug. "Love you, Maureen, and remember what I said. I'll call you tomorrow. Try to be nice."

****

As Maureen looked out over the crowd, she couldn't help noticing how everyone was coupled off. Her heart felt heavy. *Once a mean girl, always a mean girl—maybe not,* she thought. Maybe her sister was right, maybe it was time to grow up. Seeing her sister's family take leave—Kathleen snuggling her new baby while her husband, Greg, rounded up the other kids. The sting of envy burned, and she wished her life was different. *If only I could trade places with her maybe then I would feel complete and better yet, some happiness.*

Maureen sighed and turned to find Jeb Hatch, all

six-foot-one of him—wearing a scruffy two-day-old beard, wrangler jeans, and an old ripped Patriots T-shirt with what looked like grease on it—staring at her with a shit-eating grin on his face. Soaking in his ruggedly handsome face that didn't quit, and his smoking hot body she made her move. "Oh what the hell, come with me!" She grabbed him by the hand, quickly scanned the room, and calculated their escape.

"Where are we going? Food? I could use something to eat. I'm starving," he said, patting his stomach.

"Quiet," Maureen said, as she cruised them through the crowd to the back stairs. Reaching the top of the landing, she opened one of the guest rooms, pushed him inside, and turned to lock it. She faced him, stared into his unbelievable smoky gray eyes, and brushed her body up against his. Maintaining eye contact, she let her hand drop to the top button of his jeans and unbuttoned. As she did, she leaned up and gave him a quick kiss to his lips.

"Maureen," he whispered.

"Ssh," she whispered back and shimmied his jeans off.

On her tippy toes, she reached up to brush her lips against his again. With her hand to his chest, she pushed him back onto the bed. She wanted it slow and hard. Looking into his eyes, she unzipped her skirt, and let it drop to the floor. She watched the big grin spread across his face. She climbed on top of him, lowered her face to his, and kissed him slow and deep. This time letting her mouth savor. She felt his fingers brush her side as he lifted her top up and over her small, firm breasts. She released the clip from her red hair and let it cascade down over her shoulders.

Taking his hands, she placed them firmly on her hips and let herself be pulled onto him, fully straddling him, using her thighs to contract every inch. She cried out as he plunged deeper—over and over again, into her soft wet depths. Embracing every muscle, her tightness contracting, she encouraged him to set the pace, wanting it fast and fierce.

"Jeb. Oh God, Jeb."

"Maureen," he cried out.

She took him over the edge, continued to ride him until, at last, they came together with a cry, hearts pounding and bodies trembling. They held each other tight, both trying to steady the other's quake.

"I've gotta catch my breath. Jesus, Maureen, you are something else."

She fell on the bed alongside him. Her hand went to her heart to calm the pounding. He turned to look at her, a wide bashful grin spread across his face. She shifted her body to face him and smiled in return.

"I know we both probably had too much to drink," she said.

"Maureen, I haven't had a drink."

"Me either," she said and laughed.

She jumped at the sound of movement outside the door. A bit of panic spread across her face as Peter and Tom's voices echoed in the hallway. "Shit, where's my shirt?" she whispered. Her hands frantically searched through the covers on the bed. He scrambled to the floor and found her shirt by the corner post. He stood stock still with her shirt in hand.

"What are you staring at?" she demanded.

"You and your bra. I like it," he said as he handed

her the shirt.

She looked down quickly at her bra, grabbed her shirt from him, and pulled it on hastily. "Thanks, I'm leaving first, wait a few minutes before you leave the room." Before she could get away, he pulled her back toward him. She lingered in his embrace, enjoyed the feeling of his strong arms around her. She gave him a quick kiss.

"Not so fast." Pulling her back against him, he returned the kiss.

The kiss packed a punch that left her weak in the knees. "Don't do that! I've gotta be able to walk out of here." Flashing him a seductive smile, she opened the door, looked both ways down the hall, and softly closed the door after her.

Chapter 31

The next day, Jeb pulled his truck into Jack's driveway and parked. He sat behind the steering wheel and stared at the old carriage house. On the way over, he rehearsed the speech over and over in his head. Breaking the news to his best friend that he planned to date his sister was not going to be easy. He nervously tapped at the steering wheel and gazed up at the brick house and stalled. *He's going to kill me. I'm one of his best friends who's horn-dogging after his sister. Jesus, okay, okay, I can do this. If he comes after me, at least with his bum leg I can outrun him. Yes, that's a good plan. What if he fires me? Shit, I didn't think of that. I don't care. Maureen's worth it. Okay, time to man-up. Fuck me.*

"Maureen is worth an ass kicking," he said under his breath.

Taking three deep breaths, he climbed out of his truck and up the front steps. He followed the whistling and found Jack in one of the upstairs bedrooms, patching drywall.

"Hey man, you're in a good mood."

Jack glanced down from the ladder to find his best friend and smiled. "I am, it's a great day. What are you doing here?"

"I need to talk to you." Jeb dragged a nervous hand through his hair. "It's important."

"Sure, what's up Jeb-man?"

With his face poker hot, Jeb took a big breath. "I want to ask your sister out."

After a stalled silence, Jack caught Jeb's eye. "Well," he said, smirking, "you know she just had her third baby. I'm not positive, but I'm thinking maybe dating is not a big priority right now. Also, her husband might have an issue with you asking his wife out, but who am I to stand in the way of true love? I say, go for it!"

"You're a fucker, you know that man?"

"Be that as it may."

"You know I mean Maureen. I want to ask Maureen out."

Jack turned to the wall and continued patching. "Yeah, so ask her out."

"You don't care?" Jeb questioned, stunned.

"First, Maureen's a hard-ass, and—good luck with that." Jack shuddered. "If she's interested, she'll say yes, if not, she'll tell you where to go."

"But you seriously don't care?" Jeb asked in disbelief, hands on hips.

"Nope, not at all. Just one thing."

"Sure, anything."

"You start talking about sex and my sister's anatomy, I'll kill you."

"You got it, and Jack, seriously, thanks."

"Jeb, the way I see it, if one of my best friends and my sister end up hitting it off, it's a win-win all around."

"Thanks, man, I guess I could've skipped the panic attack I had in the truck."

"You might want to save those panic attacks for

when you're actually dating Maureen."

"Funny, Jack."

"You laugh now. But, seriously man, good luck, you're going need it."

Chapter 32

"Well, that oughta do it, guys," Rebecca said as she eased off the ladder, paintbrush in hand, and beamed. Accomplished, that's how she felt as she studied the side of the house with the fresh coat of baby blue paint. Satisfied with her work she wiped the paint from her hands. The air thick with the summer's heat and the physical strain of painting had sweat dripping down the side of her face and pooling under her armpits. Using the back of her hand to wipe a piece of hair plastered against her forehead, she smeared a bit of the blue paint in the process. Her pups sat under the shade of the birch tree, tongues hanging out, watching her every move. "Guys, I'm melting, how about a quick swim?"

As Rebecca turned in the direction of the pond, her dogs rose, tails wagging, and followed her as she headed down the path. At the pond's bank, she stripped out of her sticky clothes down to her underwear. She inched into the pond. The bracing cold water immediately had her body temperature plummeting. The stickiness of the day's work painting fell away, and she felt renewed and energized.

As she dipped her body deeper into the water, her head was taken up with thoughts of Polly and Silence—the sadness of their drownings—and she wondered where the truth lay. As she floated on her back with her hair fanned out around her, she delighted in the stillness surrounding her. The sunlight hot on her face being filtered through the green leaves of the trees circling the outer bank. A feeling of deep calm struck her core. *This is what I've been needing in my life. Peace.* With a couple of strong kicks, she propelled her body to the middle of the pond and floated.

Thinking of the passage from Hattie's diary about the pond, "it was hard to imagine this place filled with sadness and grief," Rebecca couldn't have agreed more. As she moved her arms through the water, an image flashed in her mind. A little girl, eyes wide, eyes panicked, a hand crushing down on her small body, forcing the child deeper under the surface of the water. She jumped slightly, feeling something brush the side of her body. She raised her head to find Manny swimming back to shore. It was then she felt the quick pull on her leg and kicked to move toward the shore. Suddenly, she stood to check her distance and felt her foot catch. Peering under the water, she located the problem—her foot lodged between two large rocks resting on the sandy bottom. She saw the figure swimming, under the water, toward her, "like a dog on a scent," getting closer and closer. The impact of the strike had her head falling below the water's surface. Struggling against the weight of the object, she yelled out for help as the water lapped slowly over her face.

****

Jack needed time to think, so he drove his truck down the backroads. He lifted his hand off the steering wheel to check his speed and thought to himself in that small movement how much he was like his father. He had seen his father make the same gesture a million times in his life, and he learned from his dad driving the backroads was a good way to clear your head. Things with Rebecca were moving fast, exciting but fast. If he was truthful with himself, it scared him a bit, actually, it scared him a lot. Jack thought of the past, loving Alice, losing Alice, and the damage it left. If he were honest with himself, he was afraid to trust in love again and scared of opening himself up to the possibility of being hurt. It was a risk he knew he needed to take. Like it or not, Rebecca was filling up the hole in his heart with love, and it scared him.

If I let fear stop me, he thought to himself, *I'll be alone for the rest of my days.* Love with Rebecca was special, boundless, and it fit. With Rebecca, he felt at home for the first time in his life. Looking at her he understood himself, the man he was and the man he could become. But most importantly, he and Rebecca were cut from the same cloth. On a whim, he turned his truck down Preston Road. He would tell her how he felt and finally let his heart do the talking.

The red luxury coupe sat in the driveway like a sore thumb and had him cursing. *What the fuck is Cam doing here?* Jack slammed his truck door and stormed toward the house. He noticed the bouquet of flowers sitting on the hood of the vehicle, wilting in the hot sun. It was then Jack heard the barking. He ran in the direction of the sound, down the path to the pond. There he found Rebecca's dogs barking and running back and forth the length of the bank. Jack sprinted toward the bank and saw Cam's arms straining to lift something out of the water. It was then Jack noticed the hair. Panic-stricken, he jumped into the water and swam out.

"Jack," Cam yelled. "I'm trying to keep her head above the water. Dive under. Something's got a hold of her leg. Hurry, I'm not sure how long I can keep this up."

With a big breath, Jack dove under the murky water. He felt his way down Rebecca's leg to her foot. With his hands, he pried the rock, freeing her foot from its prison. Breaking the surface of the water, Jack screamed, "Now! Pull!"

With each holding one of her arms, they swam and pulled her to shore. Jack laid her on the side of the bank while Cam crawled, exhausted, up the bank and sat in shock. Noticing she wasn't breathing, Jack tilted her head back and placed his mouth over hers. It didn't take long for Rebecca to cough up and vomit the swallowed water.

"Good, get it out, that's it." He held her hair back as she coughed up more water. After she finished, he eased her back to rest against him and held her. "What the hell happened out there, Cam?"

Breathing heavy, his voice filled with exhaustion, Cam began. "As soon as I got out of my car, I heard a woman screaming. I think, maybe, yelling for help. The dogs were barking. I don't know what I was thinking. I just ran and saw her in the pond. It almost looked like she was fighting something or someone off. I thought someone was in there with her, hurting her. I dove in."

"*You* dove in to save her?" Jack shouted.

"Yes," Cam, annoyed, all but yelled. "Jack, I'm aware I'm a prick, but I don't let people drown. What the fuck?" he said, resting his elbows on his knees, and breathing hard.

"Jack, Jack," Rebecca said trying to stand.

"Shh, shh, don't move...you're okay. Lie back, give it a minute, just rest." He held her tight against him and rubbed her arms to warm and steady her.

"Cam saved me," she whispered.

"I know he did, thank God. Thank God he heard you. Thank God he was here." Jack looked over at Cam. *But why was he here?*

"Jack, I was being pulled down. He was pulling me down!"

"What? Who? Cam?" Jack's voice hitched with anger.

"No, no, not Cam! Cam saved me. Someone's in the pond!" Rebecca said, agitated. Cam met Jack's eyes and shook his head no.

"Let's get you to the house." Jack cradled her in his arms and headed toward the house.

"No, Jack, something is out there. We need to check the pond."

He heard the desperate plea in her voice. He held her and placed a tender kiss on her forehead to ease her worry. "Don't worry, Cam and I will come back and check it out. I promise. Let me get you to the house first."

Chapter 33

Doc Adams gently closed the bedroom door behind him and found Jack pacing the hallway. Doc knew this look well, a man wrought with worry and scared shitless. He couldn't begin to count the number of times over the years he had seen this same expression—worry over a loved one hurt.

"How is she doing? Can I go in? Can I be with her? I need to see her," he said, his words laced with fear.

"Jack, she's exhausted, but she's going to be okay. I want you to keep an eye on her. You need to watch for signs of pneumonia and acute respiratory distress syndrome. I'm going to write this down but if you see her breathing unusually fast, acting confused, any blue tint on her lips or nails, sweat, dizziness, I want you to get her into the hospital right away. Understood?"

"Yes, yes, of course, I'll make sure."

"Jack, she is lucky you and Cam were around to save her. This could have had a very different ending. She's not out of the woods yet. So keep a close eye on her."

"I will. I need to go and be with her."

"I understand. Call me if you have any questions."

"I will and, Doc, thank you."

"You're welcome, Jack."

Doc Adams found Cam sitting at the kitchen table, a beer in his hand, his eyes vacant as he looked out over the table. "Camden?"

"Hey, sorry, Doc, I'm still a bit out of it."

"Seeing you're drinking a beer I probably don't need to check you out."

"Probably not," Cam said, shrugging his shoulders. "I'll live, Doc, thanks."

Doc Adams laid a gentle hand on Cam's shoulder and felt Cam's body jump under the unexpected touch. "You did good, Camden. You saved her. I know your father would be proud of you today, son."

"Phtt, it was impossible to make that asshole proud. Not that I give a rat's ass. In his eyes, I was always a disappointment, and he, certainly, was a disappointment to me."

"Camden, your father was a hard man who lived a hard life. It was only in the last year of his life, after he stopped drinking, that he realized how much he hurt his family. And how much he failed as a father."

"I wouldn't know about that. I never saw him after I left home at eighteen. After I left, I'd talk to my mother once in a while. I begged her to leave the bastard a million times. She never did, even though he'd beat the shit out of both of us. He was a bastard to her, a bastard to us all."

"Your mother suffered a great deal living with your father. So did you, but your father was only repeating what he knew."

"Yup, but that's no excuse, and you can't change what's been done, Doc. Water under the bridge."

"I don't believe in a family being cursed, but Cam, when it comes to your family, the heartache never ends, not even today. I think of what your mother endured, what you endured, and it breaks my heart."

"She could've left. She *chose* to stay even though he beat the shit out of me. My father was a violent drunk who destroyed everything and everyone in his path. I, for one, will never forget or forgive either one of them."

"You're right, Camden, your father was a violent drunk, but you know he came from hard circumstances."

Doc caught the eye roll, one filled with disgust.

"So did I, Doc."

"Cam, I'm not trying to make excuses for him, but you know the history, well at least some of it."

"Yeah, I know the history, well, like you said, some of it."

"History is not something you can erase, let alone forget. The last time I ran into your Uncle Issac, well let's just say, it wasn't pleasant. He, like your father, is very damaged."

"Issac? I wouldn't know. I don't care to see my own mother let alone my extended family. My motto is, break the ties the bind, choke, and kill." Cam took another long swig of his beer.

"And, Camden, how's that working for you?"

"Some days better than others."

"For my seventy-five years, I have seen a lot of hurt from the Winters' clan. I'm sorry it still continues."

"That's why I drink, Doc. Can I get you a beer?" Cam said, heading to the refrigerator.

"No thanks, I've got to get on my way. Camden, again, you did good." Doc held out his hand and pulled Cam in for a hug. He felt Cam's body jerk slightly from the touch.

188

"Thanks, Doc," Cam said, sitting back down at the table.

****

Jack entered the kitchen, to find Cam at the kitchen table. "Did Doc Adams leave?" Jack asked.

"About an hour ago. How's Rebecca doing?"

"She's asleep, exhausted, but her color is good. Lulu and the dogs are keeping watch. I plan to join them."

"Good."

"Cam, thank you for being there to save her. I know we've had our differences in the past but...thank you. I'm sorry for being a prick earlier."

Cam nodded, took another sip of his beer.

"I don't know what I would do without her." Jack's voice broke.

"Don't go there. She's going to be okay."

Jack took a long draw from the beer that Cam offered.

"Rebecca is one strong woman. You're a lucky man. She loves you. And from what I can see you love her."

"I do. I love her."

"I envy what you two have. Maybe someday, hell, maybe when I grow up," he mused.

"Cam, I owe you."

"No, Jack, you don't owe me. I've got a lot to make up for, with you, Rebecca, and I know it. I never thanked you for all the times your family took me in. Never thanked your parents for letting me stay all those times over the years, no questions asked. And I never once apologized for Alice. I'm sorry."

Jack noticed Cam's face as it clouded over.

Something in the look in Cam's eyes made Jack's heart hurt for a man who was once his best friend.

"Anyway, Jack, thanks for the extra clothes and the beer. I will make sure you get them back," Cam said and headed out the door.

Chapter 34

"Fuck," he yelled, bolting straight up in bed, hit with another panic attack. He woke up in a cold sweat, heart pounding, disoriented, and realized he was dreaming again. He rested his head in his hands, focused on his bed, his home, and what felt safe. *Another fucked up dream,* he thought to himself as he steadied his breathing.

Again, the man in all black—he's angry, holding the hand of a small child, a little girl with long blonde hair. He's pulling her arm, too rough, the snap of the bone. The little girl cries out in pain. The man doesn't stop, keeps moving down a tree-lined path that ends at a field, and beyond the field sits a pond.

Cam wondered if the characters in the dream represented him and his father. The man in black representing his father's anger and hatred of him as a son. *Best not to put too much energy into interpreting this shit. Didn't I do that enough as a child? Always wondering what was wrong with me. Why my father needed to hurt me, needed to break my bones? Always trying to be a good boy, don't get Daddy mad, blah, blah, blah.*

A shiver ran down his back as more of the dream came forward. The pond! It was Rebecca's pond, the pond she almost drowned in. And, in the dream, Cam stood on the bank with Rebecca by his side. Again, the man in black forcing the little girl into the water. *Cold, cold,* the little girl screamed. *The water's cold, Daddy!* The little girl's cries grew louder. Her crying heightened his rage until he silenced her—shaking the little girl's small body ending with a hand crushing her neck and forcing her under the cold water. *Silence. Silence. God's will.* The little girl's panic-stricken eyes, from under the water, bore into Cam's. In her eyes, he saw his own reflected back to him. Cam turned to Rebecca in the dream and screamed "Help her!" Not moving, Rebecca took his hand in hers and whispered, *It's God's will.*

In this dream like the dreams before, he was powerless. *You will always be powerless.* Cam heard the voice in his head. All he could do was stand helpless and watch the events unfold. A spectator on the shore, that's all he was. Watching a man as he drowned a little girl, whom she called Daddy. *I couldn't stop him like I couldn't stop my father.*

The phrase chanted by the man in black as he forced the child under played in Cam's head, *devil cast out, devil cast out, let the lying lips of the wicked child be put to silence.* Cam stared as the man walked past him on the bank toward the path, the man's eyes hollow. Cam turned to Rebecca again and screamed, "Why didn't you save her?" Rebecca dropped his hand, smiled sweetly, and followed the man in black up the path.

Cam reached over to his nightstand, his hands shaking. He grabbed the prescription, felt the familiar shame wash over him. He was dependent on the fucking pills to function, to control the overwhelming anxiety in his mind and body. He grabbed his water glass, swallowed the pills, sat back, and waited for the effect to take hold. Cam hit the side button on his cellphone to check the time, 5 a.m. He laid his head back on the pillow and thought of yesterday. The screams, the dog's barking, the screaming, and then, seeing Rebecca in the pond struggling for air. *Jesus,* he thought, *she almost died. Had I not gone out there...*

His truth, he had gone out to manipulate her, to fuck with her head. *What the hell is wrong with me?* He reached over, grabbed his phone, hit the contact for his mom. On the third ring, she picked up.

"Cam? Is everything okay? It's so early."

He hesitated at the sound of her voice, a groggy version of a tired voice. He couldn't recall a time that he took comfort in his mother's voice, and now it just sounded older and sadder. He wondered if he made a mistake in calling her.

"Yes," he answered coldly and thought, *you don't get more than a yes, you have no right asking if I'm okay.* He felt his body tense, the anger starting to boil. "I need—I need to get into the house, the attic. I need to put some things to rest." Cam heard her tired sigh on the other end. The long weary sigh that held years of regret, abuse, and sadness.

"Cam, there is so much you don't know. I can't tell you how ashamed I am of..."

"Mom, I didn't call to rehash the past. Just tell me where I can find the fucking key. I just need the damn key."

"Okay, Cam, but I'm not sure it's going to help you. Sometimes you have to leave well enough alone."

"I just called for the key."

"You'll find it under the gnome that sits next to the

maple tree out front. And, Cam, please don't let your Uncle Issac know you're going out to the farmhouse."

"Why?"

"Because after your father died, the farm went to Issac. And Issac made it very clear that he doesn't want any of us snooping around."

"Whatever. I didn't even know Issac was still alive."

"I haven't heard otherwise. Your father and his brother were never close, but I learned the hard way to take his threats seriously."

"If you say so."

"And Cam?"

"What?"

He waited, heard his mother's labored breathing. "I'm sorry. I should've left. I should've saved us both," and with her words, he hung up the phone.

Chapter 35

East Hill Road was a class four dirt road with little traffic except for farmers with equipment traveling to and fro. As Cam headed down the dusty, rutted road, he thought about all the time he walked East Hill as a child. The stench of manure filled his nostrils, suffocating, so he always tried to breathe through his mouth. As Cam walked the mile to the farm, he'd plan his escape. He was masterful at crafting elaborate plans to end his parents and run away.

His favorite one involved killing his parents while they slept and then escaping to South America to be a drug lord. God, how he dreamed of being someone different, someone powerful, that others admired. He figured, over the years he crafted millions of plans to kill his parents, and sometimes, even though he hated to admit it, some of his plans included killing himself. As he drove, Cam thought of how much he despised East Hill Road, every dirty and dusty inch of it, and yet he needed to come back here to understand—back to the place where it all began.

Cam sat in his car and looked up at the decaying farmhouse with its missing front steps where he spent his childhood. The memories came flooding back, and the pit in his stomach grew. *Do I really need to do this?* Cam heard his father's voice ring in his ears. *Come on, you pussy. I dare you.* Cam tried to control the tremble in his hands. *What would he find today? Sober, angry father or drunken, violent father.* "You're fucking dead!" he shouted, hitting the steering wheel with his fists.

With years of practice, Cam had acquired a repertoire of coping skills. Today, at this moment, he chose one of his childhood favorites, an oldie but a goodie—the trick of breathing and counting silently in his head, an exercise he used as he opened his car door and stood at the ready to face his demons.

He located the key under the gnome, took another deep breath, and put the key in the door. He knew he would need to put some weight behind the door to open it to combat the years of trapped humidity. If memory served, it always swelled more in the summer's heat. As the door gave way, his heart squeezed, being crushed in the vise that was his family home.

The stench of the house hit Cam like a sucker punch to the gut, a stale combination of mildew, years of smoking, and rancid burnt grease. The smell clung to everything, a permanent reminder of all the despair the house contained. Cam blew out a breath to steady himself and thought how he always hated the dank smell of the old place. He'd vowed that when he got older, he would live in a sterile environment, the polar opposite of the filth that he came from. His eyes followed the path of the black mold spreading on the walls and ceiling like a cancer.

As a child, he thought dying might be the best kept secret of them all. That dying was the only way out. A way to finally be at peace and, maybe, ultimately, happy. Eyeing the large cookstove in the kitchen, the memory came back. One of Cam's favorite plans formed while his father held his hand over an open flame. He'd burn the house down while his parents slept upstairs—he'd stand on the front lawn and watch, basking in the beauty of the flames. The home engulfed in a bright blaze of fury. The satisfaction in finally taking control and the joy in hearing his parents scream for help, knowing that no one would answer their cries. Like no one answered his, justice served at last.

He'd set the fire only when his father was passed out. The only downfall in the plan was there would be no satisfaction in hearing his father cry out to Cam for help. This always brought him a sense of disappointment. He wanted his father to pay. Wanted to see the panic in his father's eyes and the knowledge that his son finally took control and ended it. *Not a pussy after all, huh, Dad.* His fantasies sustained his existence, each day thinking to himself after a beating—*this could be the day*. Cam had meticulously detailed every plan in a journal but never, ever, had the courage to actually follow through with one. *Maybe my father was right. Maybe I am a pussy.*

As Cam moved through the kitchen, he noticed a field mouse scurrying between the floorboards and found it ironic that something could still be alive in the old house. He actually felt sorry for the mouse, stuck in this hell hole. As he continued through the house, he noticed the furniture in the adjoining room covered in linens and coated in a thick layer of dust. He placed his hand on the railing and immediately pulled back his hand, wiping a grayish-black residue of old dust off on one leg his khakis. He made his way up the first long staircase to the bedrooms.

As he reached the top landing, the terror bubbled

over. He knew it wasn't rational, but he believed the house knew he was back home. The walls of the house breathed him in, trying to claim the remainder of his soul. With his chest tightening, he knew he needed to hurry and get out as quickly as possible. Evil lurked even in an empty house.

He passed the door to his childhood bedroom on the right. His room was directly across the hall from his parents. A feeling of dread hit him like a truck, the terror crushing his limbs. He didn't dare look into either room, convinced he would see that little boy huddled under the bed, hiding from the monster. Cam knew monsters were real and that hiding was the only option, even if it was futile.

The story of his childhood went by like a picture reel in slow motion. He'd lived the horror film, always one of the lead characters. It always started with Cam's father, drinking and raging at his mother, striking her with his fists over and over again—the blood, the smell of booze, and the screams. Always threatening to get the gun, to end her. The final scene was always the same, his father threatening to kill his mother and then himself as Cam hid under his bed, shaking, plastering his little body against the wall. With eyes tightly shut, his little mind believing if he closed them tight enough his father wouldn't be able to see him. After a while, Cam started praying that his father would follow through and kill them all. *Peace, finally peace.*

He tried to block the memories as he continued to climb another set of stairs to the attic. He looked up the stairs and saw his father's angry face peering down at him. Again, his father's voice in his head. *C'mere, dumb ass. You crying like a pussy again, boy?* He knew his mind was playing tricks on him. He knew his father was dead. He closed his eyes, and when he looked up, his father was gone, replaced by the lone wooden door. The crimson door that used to make him pee himself as a child. He paused on the stairs to breathe, practiced slowing his heart rate, and then he smelled it. The stench of bourbon and stale beer. *Stop it. It's not real. They're just memories. He's dead!*

He heard the pleas of the little boy as his drunk father dragged the boy's body up the stairs. He flashed back on all the times his father forced him into the room behind the red door. The attic where his father would beat him, tie him up, and use him for target practice. His small voice begging for his mother to save him, pleading for her to come, but she never did. He'd listen under the door as his father stumbled drunk down the steps, and prayed to God that, this time, his father would fall and break his neck.

Cam reached into his pocket, took out the vial of pills he always carried with him. The "just in case" pills, to calm his racing heart. He placed two of the tablets under his tongue, closed his eyes for a moment to feel the relief, and opened the door. He found the trunk quickly in the back corner of the room. Knew exactly where he'd find the yellowed pages of the diary.

The first diary that recorded his family's history, the history of trauma and abuse. He grabbed it and fled, not even bothering to lock the door behind him. Sprinting to his car, he jumped in and locked the doors. He was safe. Cam rubbed his hands on his pants to steady the shaking and took one last look at the house. *I should've burned it down. I should've killed us all when I had the chance.* And he vowed to himself never to return.

****

Cam came to, hunched over the steering wheel, in his driveway. He had no idea how long he'd been sitting there. The drive home had been a blur. Looking up at his house, he felt safe. He looked at the diary, wrapped up in the brown leather binding, sitting next to him in the passenger seat. A wave of doubt skimmed just under the surface of his mind. *What am I doing? Is reading this really going to help bring closure?* Something in his head and body had him doubting it.

Chapter 36

Once inside the house, he sat at the kitchen table and poured a tall glass of 21-year-old scotch. He placed the bottle next to the glass. He picked up the diary, ran his fingers across the smooth brown leather case. Inside sat the yellowed pages bound together with string, worn from age. He picked up his glass and took a generous sip. The slow burn of the liquor caressed him, better than any lover he ever had. His chest rose with a deep breath. He took a minute to savor the Chivas and began to read.

Diary of Cyrene Winters

"July 1st, 1788. The trip down from Canada was long, the buggy was wet and sticky with humidity. I am weary to the bone. I am to marry John Winters in a month. I am staying at John's aunt's home in Cambridge, Vermont, until the wedding. John's parents own the biggest dairy farm in Eden. The plan is for John and me to farm the land adjacent to his parents. I am homesick for Quebec, for Canada, and I miss my parents and sister terribly. My heart has such sorrow, but know I am making a necessary sacrifice for my family. John promises that as soon as possible, we will send for my parents and sister to live with us."

"October 4th, 1788. I fear I am with child. I wish I was joyful but feel stuck in my misery. I have no feeling for this man whom I am to call Husband. When I

inquired about my parents and sister coming down from Quebec, Husband became angry. He said my attention should be only on him and that I may not speak of my family until he has news. I fear he plans to keep me ignorant in regards to delivering my family. My heart is heavy. It pleased him to hear that I am with child."

"June 7th, 1789. I am having difficulty moving with my legs swollen twice their size. Husband is displeased with my work and punished me. My clothing sufficiently hides the bruises that I know will appear like the others before. I cry most days and nights, longing for my parents and sister whom I have not seen or heard from since I arrived. I feel nothing for this baby inside me and wish to escape from this farm, from Husband, from my hell."

"July 4th, 1789. After a long labor with Husband's mother in attendance. I gave birth to twins, twin boys, the first, Husband named Hiram, exalted one, and he named the other Adly, given his small stature. Husband is pleased that I gave him sons and he deemed that Hiram will be a Reverend. I feel nothing for these babies and refuse to hold them. I feel that I must take some rest. Husband had his mother tarry over to care for the babies."

"August 6th, 1789. Husband has taken a keen interest in Hiram, spends little time holding Adly, who is a sickly baby. I'm afraid that Hiram took more than his fair share from his brother and is at fault for making his brother sickly."

"September 21st, 1794. I'm very much fatigued, large with child, I went out to the barn to tell Husband to fetch his mother now that my water broke. I left Adly at the table with his drawings. Looking through the

window of the barn I saw Husband doing unspeakable things. Hiram struggling against the weight of his father, Hiram looked right at me through the window. No tears just a strange expressionless face. I felt nothing watching Husband hurting Hiram. I turned to go back to the house to put the fire on."

"September 26th, 1794. I gave birth to a baby girl, a sweet babe, I named her Caroline, she seems to have awoken me from my spell. She is a cute little thing with tufts of blonde hair. Husband is angry to have a girl who in his eyes is a worthless feeder on a farm. Hiram refuses to look at Caroline, but Adly is fascinated by his little sister."

"November 15th, 1795. I gave birth to another girl, I named her Evelyn. Husband looked at her, grunted, and took leave. Husband is displeased."

"November 26th, 1795. I found Evelyn dead in her crib. Husband said it was for the best. In my mind's eye I know this baby died at the hands of Husband. The hatred I feel in my heart grows each day. I overheard Sadie Mitchell speaking about a woman in the next village over who knows how to end being with child with a mixture of black cohosh and evening primrose herbs. I will pay her a visit when I go for provisions next week."

"September 12th, 1797. I gave birth to another boy, Samuel. I fear myself greatly. The thoughts I have toward this baby are not motherly and am wrestling with strong desires to go astray. My thoughts are not my own and know the workings of the devil. God help me! Husband took the baby to his mother. I felt relieved fearing I would harm the infant. Sweet Adly hasn't left

my bedside, and Caroline is a mother's hen."

"April 29th, 1807. I killed Husband today. I hit him squarely on the head with the spade from the barn as he sat at the kitchen table in one of his fits. Hiram helped me drag his body to the hay barn. His brother, Adly, is too tender for such work, so I sent him to watch the road. Hiram helped me set the hay barn on fire. I gathered the children and set off into the woods in search of fiddleheads. Upon our return, it seemed that the whole village worked to extinguish the blaze. I wailed for Husband and dropped to my knees. Persis Post sat in wait with me until Alvan Hyde of the Hyde farm informed me that Husband's body was found badly burned and that he was dead. Now I expect a bit more cheerfulness in my life knowing Husband will be ripe for hell."

He closed the diary and poured himself another tall scotch. He gazed at the amber liquid, his seductress, as stories spun in his head. The hush whispers molded his family system, and there was no escape from their power. The patriarch, John, with a long history of sexual abuse, his suspected delusional thinking, cruelty, violence, and alcoholism. He heard all the rumors of generational abuse and felt that it permeated his skin, echoing in his cells, in his DNA. All of which was kept alive, like a beating heart, by town gossips. Now, another story, one of Cyrene Winters and her side of crazy. He felt disgusting at his core and reached for his glass. His favorite coping skill that never disappoints. The slow burn from the scotch eased the sense of doom he felt in his bones. And he hoped it would continue to provide the necessary distraction from his thoughts and feelings. *Not enough scotch on the planet for that,* he thought as he rubbed his throbbing temples.

"Enough," he screamed as he placed his head in his hands. The drumming behind his eyes and in his head grew louder. The voices demanding to be heard. *It's time, boy, time to claim your birthright.* He reached in his pocket for his vial—not enough pills to end it, but enough to lessen the pain and quiet his head. He swallowed three down with the rest of the scotch and took solace in the knowledge that soon he'd be numb.

Chapter 37

As she gazed out over the pond, the stillness of the water eased Rebecca's troubled mind. With the comfort of her dogs who sat alongside her, she tried to recall yesterday's events. She was relieved to finally be alone after talking a reluctant Jack into going to work. His cellphone had buzzed all morning, a clear indication that he had work to look after. She overheard Jack talking to Carol about the near drowning, and frustration filled her. She was fine. Her body ached, but her head was clear.

As she headed out to the woods for a walk with her dogs, she'd worked to clear the worried thoughts from her head. Max stopped at the base of the tree, sniffing excitedly. Manny ran up and joined him.

"Come on, you two!" she said, urging the dogs to follow her. Her dogs sat at command at the base of the tree and started to whine. "What is it?" It was then she noticed the tree stand midway up the tree. Cigarette butts littered the ground. "Ah, hunters, looks like we're going to need to post the land, guys." She patted their heads. "Let's go home."

Emerging from the woods, she stopped in her tracks and turned back toward the pond. The picture of Cam in the water filled her head. Maybe he could help her. Perhaps he could fill in some of the missing pieces. Rebecca decided to text Jack, let him know she was going to visit Cam. Explain that she needed Cam's guidance to fill in the blank spots. Most of all she needed to thank him in person for saving her from drowning. Rebecca called to her dogs and headed home.

Opening the door to the mudroom, Rebecca heard the familiar ringtone that was her mother's. "Hi, Mom!" She worked to keep her voice steady, even happy. On the other end, her mother exhaled and let out an audible sigh of relief.

"What happened? I know something happened so, just tell me," her mother demanded.

Rebecca smiled. Her mother's instinct was spot on when it came to her kids.

"I'm fine, Mom, just a bit of a mishap at the pond. I went out for a quick dip and..." Rebecca paused, knew she was bending the truth a bit to ease her mother's worry, "my foot became lodged between a couple of rocks, and, thank God, Jack and my realtor, Cam Winters, were there to help me."

She heard the familiar creak of her mother's rocking chair. A flash of an image crossed Rebecca's eyes. A picture of her at age five sitting with her mom on that very rocker being rocked back and forth—a nightly ritual for the two of them. At that moment, Rebecca wished she was once again five and could climb up on her mother's warm lap, to be held and comforted.

"You're sure you're okay?" her mother asked, a skilled detective at uncovering the truth.

Rebecca steadied her voice, knowing if it cracked her mom would turn up the level of concern, and the tears would flow.

"I'm okay. Just a bit shaken up, nothing that a good night's sleep didn't cure."

"How about I come up? I want to put my eyes on my baby girl. I could make a pot roast, or maybe a hearty soup. I'll cook all your favorites and, maybe, even some of those ginger cookies you like so much."

Rebecca closed her eyes and could almost smell the ginger filling her house. The childhood memory, coming in the front door after a long day at school. Her senses hit by the comforting smells of her mom's cooking. The constant that made everything and everyone feel safe and warm.

"Mom, that would be great but right now is not…."

"Rebecca, the whole family would like to come for a visit. Your brothers were talking about surprising you. You know how they worry. I told them to hold off. Saying we probably should check in with you first. Your dad wants to bring you some tools. We all want to help with the house, and, of course, all of us want to meet Jack."

Rebecca smiled at the thought of her whole family storming her home. Her nieces and nephews running around the yard—picking berries, hiking, helping her stack wood. Her brothers and father would stand in the front yard picking apart her home, and, of course, picking apart Jack. She expected her brothers to give her the hard time that was par for the course being a little sister. The whole family would provide her loads of unwanted constructive criticism about her house and the work the house needed. She also knew her brothers would give Jack the third degree and, when or if he passed, would welcome him with open arms.

She wasn't ready for the onslaught of her family

quite yet and also knew she needed to be careful not to hurt her mother's feelings. Family dynamics were always hard to navigate even when her family remained her compass. The knowing in her heart that her family was still there brought Rebecca comfort like a warm cup of tea on a cold day.

"Mom, you know I can't wait for you all to visit, but right now I have a crew of workers out here. I'm planning a housewarming party in early October and plan to have all of you up then." Rebecca rubbed her hand over her heart knowing her mother did the same.

"You know, Rebecca, you'll always be my baby. I don't care how old you get. I will always worry about my baby girl."

"I know, Mom. I'll call you later this week, and we'll look at the calendar together. You can help me choose the date for the housewarming. How does that sound?"

"All right dear, if that's what you want," her mother said, her voice filled with resignation.

The guilt in hurting her mother's feelings was palpable. "I love you, Mom."

"I love you too, honey."

"We'll talk soon. Love to Dad. Bye, Mom."

"Bye, honey."

As Rebecca hung up, she typed in her text to Jack.

Chapter 38

Jack sat, preoccupied, at the large conference room table at Corcoran and Sons. He barely listened to his father and Jeb as they fought about the budget for the McKenzie project. The picture of a struggling Rebecca in the pond had him scattered and fully distracted him from paying attention to what was going on around him. He glanced at the clock on the wall, tapped the table with his pen, and glanced at the clock again. He was relieved to excuse himself when his phone vibrated. Stepping out into the hall, he caught the last remnants of his father and Jeb's debate over the number of drywall suppliers. He'd heard this debate before and had no use for it today. He checked his phone as the second text lit up the screen.

J. —*Going to c Cam, need answers & need to thank him in person. If u r in town can you meet me at his place? R. By the way,i love you. Heart emoji. R.*—

"Shit," he said under his breath. Going back into the conference room, Jack couldn't hide his worry.

"Problem, son?" Henry said as Jack gather his things off the table and headed toward the door.

"Nothing I can't handle. I will check in with you guys when I'm done. And, in my opinion, I'd go with Simon's drywall, better quality and more expensive but worth it in the end. Plus the McKenzie family has more money than they know what to do with."

****

As Rebecca drove into the village, she turned left onto Main Street. Cam built his house in the exclusive neighborhood that housed the original homes built in Eden. During the closing, she'd sat in his house many times—a modern construction with clean lines and minimalist elements. The glass house stood out like a sore thumb in a neighborhood filled with old craftsman-style homes. She wondered if it was Cam's way of saying, *"fuck you"* to his neighbors and all of Eden— *I'm nothing like you, and leave me the fuck alone.* Like the house, Cam did his best to stand out and took pride in the fact that he was different. And Rebecca knew there was a reason for that.

She walked the stone pathway lining the side of the house to the backdoor, where Cam's office was located, and knocked. From inside the house, she heard a loud crash. Peering through the side window, she caught sight of a foot and knocked again.

"Cam?" Rebecca called out as she opened the door. She found him splayed out on the kitchen floor. An empty, broken scotch bottle sat next to him. Pieces of broken glass littered the counter and the ceramic floor around him. His right hand bore a deep cut with blood seeping into the yellowed pages of a diary he clutched in the same hand. Wetting a paper towel, she crouched down on the ceramic tile to inspect his wound.

"Cam, I'm going to clean your hand. Okay?"

"I can't stop the dreams. Please help stop the dreams," he pleaded.

"Let me get you cleaned up." Removing the pages, she inspected the wound and pulled out a single shard of glass. She located a first aid kit in the downstairs bathroom. As she tended to the cut, she heard Jack's truck pull up.

He found her on the kitchen floor bandaging Cam's hand. "What the hell happened in here?"

"I'm not sure, but one thing is for sure, he's wasted. He did a real number on his hand. I finally got the bleeding under control."

"How can I help?"

"Can you help me get him to bed?"

Jack hoisted Cam to his feet, swung his arm around him, and all but dragged him into the bedroom.

"Jack, Jack, help me st-stop the dreams," Cam slurred.

"Sure, Cam, don't worry, we got you."

Rebecca left them in the bedroom. Jack found her sitting on the kitchen floor, reading from the pages.

"What is all of this?" He said, crouching next to her on the floor.

"Jack, this is Cyrene Winters' diary. This page here…" She shifted her body so Jack could read alongside her. "This is the page that Cam was holding when I found him. Cyrene writes that her son, the Reverend Winters, drowned his wife and child in the pond. He confessed to his mother. She knew her son killed them, and she protected him. She knew the truth."

Jack looked over Rebecca's shoulder to the diary.

"She knew her son drowned his wife and her granddaughter in the pond behind my house."

"And she protected him?"

"Yes."

"What the hell do we do with this? We're talking about a crime that occurred over 150 some years ago," he said.

"I'm not sure, but this story needs to be told. Polly and Silence want their truth to be known. The dreams, the giggling, appearing in my goddamn kitchen, I just…"

"And the near drowning? Was that part of getting your attention?" he said, his voice full of spite.

"Jack, all I know is they're trying very hard to open my eyes to what happened at that pond. Maybe Polly and Silence need justice to move forward and to be at peace."

"How? What's justice? He can't be charged. And peace? They're all dead."

"I don't know. I need to figure out how to help them. Maybe in exposing the truth about what happened at that pond will provide them with some closure."

"What do you mean?" Jack asked.

"When I arrived, Cam kept muttering about…something about stopping the dreams. I think Cam is part of this."

"He was saying the same to me in the bedroom. He was begging me to help him stop the dreams."

"I wonder what else this diary reveals about the Winters family. I need to find Carol and talk to her." Rebecca began to pick up the loose pages of the diary.

"She's probably still at the library. Are you taking the diary?"

"Yes, I'll be back, maybe in a couple of hours. Can you handle things here?"

"Yeah, I got it. Actually, I'd like to stay and make sure he's okay. I guess old habits die hard."

"Yet another reason I love you." She embraced

him, placing her head against his heart for just a moment. "I'll be back soon."

"You know where to find me. I love you, Rebecca."

"I love you too."

****

Rebecca found Carol reading in the library stacks.

"Hey, Rebecca, I am reading the most interesting research on the epigenetic transmission of trauma. It says here that a single episode of trauma can alter the genetic makeup, not just in the individual, but their children, grandchildren, and great-grandchildren. Makes me think of our research and the clan Winters."

"Do you have a private office where we can talk?"

"Of course. We can use one of the study rooms."

Carol led Rebecca to a small conference room to the right of the stacks and unlocked the door. Rebecca spread the pages of the diary on the small table in front of them.

"What's all this?" Carol asked.

"This is Cyrene Winters' diary."

"How did you...?" Carefully, Carol opened the diary and read the first entry. She stopped and studied Rebecca. "Where did you get this? Is this blood?" Carol sniffed at the page.

"I just came from Cam's house. I went over to thank him for saving me. I found him on the floor, drunk, with the diary scattered around him and, yes, that's Cam's blood on the pages."

"This is incredible."

"I know. I'm desperate to understand what's going on. From what I read, Cyrene Winters knew that her son was responsible for drowning his wife and daughter in the pond. Her son confessed, and she protected him. She kept it quiet."

"So, he was responsible. Our gut feelings about the Reverend were correct. I wonder what other secrets this diary contains? What else did Cyrene write about? Let me get my laptop and let's get to work."

As Carol went to retrieve her computer, Rebecca said a prayer for peace for Polly and Silence, knowing that she and Carol were closer to the truth.

Chapter 39

Cam knew the faces all too well in his dream. His father holding a gun to his son's head, his breath reeking of alcohol, and with him—the man in black. Cam heard his father's voice in his head, the voice of his abuser, "Boy, you should've let her drown, now you'll have to pay." His father held the gun on him while the man in black removed his belt. The sound of the belt snapping had his chest pounding, the strike against his back had him screaming, falling out of bed and crawling to hide.

"Cam, you're okay. It's just a dream. Hey, hey, it's Jack. You're okay." Jack helped him up off the floor.

Cam woke, disoriented, and rubbed his heart to calm the explosion in his chest. The pounding from his heart reverberated in his head. His body was soaked with sweat, and he feared he might have pee'd himself. Unsettled still, he tried to slow his breathing. He tasted the acidy bile in his throat and struggled to speak.

"Where am I?"

"Home, in your bedroom. You were having a nightmare. I came in because I heard you screaming and found you on the floor."

"How'd you get here? Why are you here?"

"Rebecca texted me that she was coming over to talk to you about what happened at the pond and to thank you. She asked me to meet her here."

"Rebecca? Is she here?"

"No, she's not."

He sat down next to Cam on the edge of the bed.

"I'm okay, now. You can leave," he said dismissively. A master at putting up walls to keep people out. *Hell,* he thought, *I've been doing it for years.*

"I know you're okay. Why don't you take a shower? And when you're done, meet me in the kitchen. I'll have some coffee and toast waiting for you."

Not having any energy to put up a fight, he gave in. "Okay, Jack."

"I'll try to explain what Rebecca wanted to talk to you about once you've showered."

"All right," he said, with his heart clenched in his chest. *Fuck, here we go again.* With Jack out of the room, he swallowed another anti-anxiety pill and headed to the bathroom to wait for the release.

Cam spent a long time under the hot water. He tried his best to scald away the remainder of the dream from his brain and his body. The medicine was barely taking the edge off. In his heart, he knew his story could never change. His family tree would always be a fucked-up mixture of backwoods sociopaths. He'd spent a lifetime trying to wash away the shame.

With his hand, he felt around his back, expecting to find raised welts from the belt. The sensation of a beating that never occurred remained, his body remembered and still responded. The only difference this time was that he wasn't a small, helpless child trying to cover up the abuse, but now rather a grown man that needed pills and booze to deal with the aftermath. *The apple doesn't fall far from the tree.*

Freshly showered and sitting back on his bed, he reached again for his prescription. He prayed that he could get the shaking in his hands under control before seeing Jack again. *Dig deep, you pussy, get a hold of yourself. Shut the fuck up, Dad.* Cam swore at his body for betraying him, outing him for being weak, and failing to hide how fucked up he really was.

Chapter 40

Rebecca squeezed her eyes shut and waited for Carol to finish reading. They'd just spent the last two hours poring over the diary's contents.

"Carol, from these accounts, it's pretty clear that John and Cyrene Winters were quite disturbed."

"More like complete sociopaths."

"Clearly, Cyrene Winters was broken. Her life with John Winters broke her. The abuse to her and her children, the isolation from her family, and being trapped. Her description of killing her husband was chilling, absolutely no remorse," Rebecca pondered.

"She was finally free. Given the years of abuse she and her children endured and, also, suspecting her husband killed one of her babies. I can understand why she did it. My only question, what took her long?" Carol wondered.

"I'm sure she spent years fantasizing ways to kill him."

"Yup, just waiting for the opportunity to present itself. I wonder what Cam and his relatives make of their family history? To come from all this darkness. How does one reconcile such a sad legacy?"

"From what I witnessed today, it's clear Cam isn't coming to terms with his past. I keep thinking about Polly and Silence. What do they want? And why do they keep showing up? Why now? For Cam?"

"I wish I knew, Rebecca.

"There's a message behind what Polly and Silence are showing me. Truthfully, Carol, at this point, I would settle for peaceful coexistence in the cape. Much like Cam, I need the dreams to stop."

"Both you and Cam are having dreams. Our next step should be sitting down with him. We need to get his perspective and listen to what he has to say. Maybe after talking with Cam, we'll know what to do next."

"By the way, do you know if Cam has other living relatives in the area?"

"Well, I know Cam has a mother, but she moved down south after Cam's dad died. And I believe he has an uncle, his father's older brother, Issac, who lives somewhere in Belvedere—that is, if he's still alive."

"I wonder if Cam is in contact with him?"

"I don't know. Over the years, there's been plenty of rumors about Issac Winters."

"Rumors?"

"Rumors about domestic violence, illegal selling of firearms, even poaching moose and deer off-season. I think he even went so far as trying to sell moose meat, which is illegal. Now that I think about it, I remember reading a story in the local newspaper about Issac entering the courthouse with a rifle. He made threats against one of the probate judges. I think he served some time in jail for that stint," Carol mused.

"Sounds like an interesting character. I suppose it's worth a shot. He might be able to shed some light."

"Maybe."

"I'm going to text Jack and let him know we are heading over. Cam might be a bit worn and hungover, but he might be willing to talk to us."

For a moment, Rebecca thought of the weight of Cam's burden, knowing all too well the echoes of unresolved trauma and the toll on the soul. From her own experience, trying to shove away trauma was useless, and her heart broke for him.

Chapter 41

Entering through the side door, Carol and Rebecca found Cam and Jack at the kitchen table drinking coffee. Jack smiled up as they entered and motioned for them to take a seat.

"We came back to return the diary," Carol said, as she placed the diary in front of them. Cam sat with eyes fixed on his coffee and nodded.

"I'm sorry I took the diary without asking you first. I need your help, Cam," Rebecca said, putting a hand to his forearm and fixing her eyes on his.

His head jerked up at the feel of her touch and the sound of her voice, and he met her gaze. He saw it then, the signs of torment, the dark circles, and the shakiness in her voice. He knew, like himself, she was struggling and, like him, was likely being haunted.

"How?" His voice cracked in response, and he searched her face in hopes that she knew the answer.

"I don't know, but like you, Cam, I need it to stop. Since I moved into the house your ancestor built, dreams have plagued my sleep. We're connected in some way."

"I know," Cam said.

"How do you know?" she asked.

"Don't ask me how but I think I've entered some of your dreams and you mine."

"I think you're right. There's a name for it—it's

called psychic dreaming."

"But, how?"

"The house and your ancestors are the bridge or what's linking our dreams together."

"I wish I'd never sold you that damn house. I should've torched it and burned all of this with it to the ground," he said, motioning to the diary.

"I think the dreams are trying to tell us something. But like you, I need the dreams to stop. I want my life back."

"Okay, but I don't know what I can do. How can I help?" Cam felt the shame in his chest, one of powerlessness, like that small child who wished and prayed the bad away.

"Cam, Rebecca and I wondered if talking to your other relatives, getting their perspective might be useful," Carol said.

"How? What do you expect to learn? Do you think they're having dreams too?"

"Truthfully, we don't know. It's a bit like grasping at straws. I remember your Uncle Issac. I think he used to live in Belvedere," Carol said.

"Issac? I haven't seen him in years. Last I heard he was living on the side of a mountain and, you're right, it was in Belvedere. He's always been a bit of a recluse."

"Yes, but he is your only living relative on your father's side. Correct?"

"Yes, my father had only the one brother."

"Well, he might also be struggling and, maybe, just maybe, he'll have answers for us," Rebecca added.

Cam listened to Rebecca's words and considered. "I suppose it's worth trying. I can call my mother and see if she knows how to reach him."

"If your uncle is willing to talk to us, Carol and I thought he might be more comfortable with a local. Carol is willing to go with you."

"Right now, I think my body would benefit from more sleep. I will let you guys find your way out," he said, standing. "Carol, I'll be in touch."

Chapter 42

Issac Winters' sixty-year-old knees ached as he made his way farther up the mountainside from his cabin. He stopped to catch his breath, leaned against a poplar tree to rest, and raised his canteen to his lips. He looked up to the sky, sniffed the crisp air, and smelled the coming snow. It wasn't unusual to get a bit of snow in late September in the mountains. He inhaled another big breath of air and heard the call of a turkey in the distance. He loved the isolation up here—he never cared much for people. In his opinion, people were more trouble than they were worth, always poking their heads into things that were none of their business. A big reason he kept to himself, lived on a mountainside, and rarely felt a need to come off it.

Issac trudged through the mountainside covered in dense woods, moving through the forest with precision, checking each trap, and frustrated to find them empty. Issac was well aware that the city dwellers below made a fuss about baiting traps, but nobody dared to challenge him. Everything he caught, he ate, even the occasional dog. Truth be told, he didn't give a rat's ass what people thought of him; it was his land, and he'd do what he pleased on it.

Reaching his lookout point, Issac caught wind of the faint whine. Something was dying, and he followed the sound. He fished a cigarette that he stowed behind his right ear and lit it. He located the coyote in an old rusted steel trap at the edge of his property line. The coyote lay with glazed-over eyes and a body exhausted from struggle. Taking a long drag off the cigarette, he sat back to watch death take hold.

When the coyote's eyes fell shut, he kicked at its body. Saw the coyote's body twitch and knew that death was not far. Issac preferred the eyes open, peering up at him, pleading. It always aroused him to see those pleading eyes one last time. He'd learned at an early age that death and sex were intimately linked. Hell, his own father taught him how to tie a rope around his neck when he touched himself. It was a balancing act; he'd learned quickly not to be too greedy with pleasure.

The smell of death was a sexual bouquet to him unlike any he had ever known—not a stench but a welcome enticement. He flicked the cigarette aside and with the palm of his hand, he quieted his hard-on.

He raised the butt of his gun and slammed it down. *Dinner.*

As he made his way back to his cabin, Issac grimaced at the sight of the fancy foreign-made car parked in front of the cabin, a red luxury coupe. He swore under his breath, "damn leaf peepers," every year the same thing—the onslaught of the out-of-state visitors vacationing to catch peak foliage. *What didn't they understand?* There was a reason he lined his woods with "No Trespassing" signs. Knowing he gave fair warning, he smirked. *"Violators will be shot."* He ran his hand down the butt of his rifle, at the ready. This he would enjoy. He could already hear the story in his head. *Remember the time we drove up the class four road and that crazy guy pulled the gun on us in the*

226

middle of the woods when we stopped to ask for directions. I thought we'd never get out of there alive. He found them, deep in conversation, their eyes locked on each other. The young girl, big eyes like a doe, blue in color though, not brown. She looked up at the male, expectantly, eager, her mouth moving fast. They never heard him approach.

"Hands at your side, don't move unless your head is bulletproof," Issac warned. He snickered as the two jumped at the sound of his warning.

And laughed a full belly laugh as the young man raised his hands in surrender.

"Uncle Issac, I'm your nephew, Camden Winters, your brother's son, and this is my friend, Carol Mahoney."

"My brother's dead. He was a weak man who died from the drink."

"Yeah, I know. Nonetheless, I'm his son. My mother gave me directions to your cabin. She didn't have a number for you. She wasn't sure you were still alive."

"I'm alive, boy. What do you want?"

"We were wondering if we could talk to you?"

"About what, boy?"

"Family history. We won't take much of your time."

Issac stood, stock still and considered. He studied them, waited for the "tells" in their body language like he would a buck waiting to be taken until, at last, satisfied he'd finish the kill.

"Well, don't just stand there, come on in."

Chapter 43

As they followed Issac into the dark cabin, Carol
and Cam were struck by the smell. A vile stench, what
smelled like a combination of urine, old cigarettes,
blood, and rotting meat. The cabin was sparsely
furnished: an old brown corduroy recliner, patched with
duct tape, sat in the corner; next to the recliner, sat a
small table with a lantern. On the windowsill, a series
of mason jars were filled to the brim with old cigarette
butts. An oversized wood stove dominated the room. In
the corner off to the side of the stove was a pile of
neatly stacked wood. A kitchenette, off the main living
area, held a small butcher block table, a side counter
with a small sink, and a wood cook stove. All of which
could be seen through the doorway.

Issac slammed the coyote on the butcher block
table, grabbed a knife, and peeled a portion of the hide
back.

"Whew, that's a ripe one," Issac said, taking a big
breath.

The smell of blood filled the room. Carol reached
for Cam's arm.

"Are you okay?" he asked, watching as her face
collapsed.

She nodded and covered her nose with the palm of
her hand.

"Never smelled a fresh kill, girlie?" Issac grunted.

"No, I can't say I have," she choked out. "I'll be fine. I'm just sensitive to smells."

"Phht, this ain't the Ritz, dear. A man has to eat."

"Uncle Issac, Carol didn't mean to offend you. We can wait outside if you would rather."

Afraid she was going to vomit, Carol moved toward the front of the cabin. She caught a movement out the front window and turned to Cam.

"Smell getting to you too, boy? Hell, the smell of this blood is making me hungry. You two can stay for dinner if you'd like. I'll have this coyote in the frying pan in no time." Issac wiped the fresh blood dripping from his hands onto his pants and sneered. "It's true, you know, what they say."

"What's true Uncle Issac?"

"Everything tastes like chicken. Your father never had the stomach for it either. He was no hunter. He couldn't track a damn thing even if it left a bloody trail. He was a pathetic excuse for a man. I don't mean to speak ill of the dead, just speaking the truth that's all. You hunt, boy?"

"No, I don't hunt, Uncle Issac."

"Of course you don't. Did your father ever tell you about the time I hunted him? Fucking hilarious, the sight your father, pee'd his britches and crying like a baby when I found him—pitiful."

"That sounds terrifying, Uncle Issac."

"Oh come on, now, just two brothers having a little fun in the woods. Nothing to worry your pretty little head about, boy."

Issac moved from the kitchen, his eyes traveling over Carol's face. "You look like her, you know."

"Like who?" Confused, Carol tilted up her chin and

faced him.

"Wait here. I have a photo, the only photo ever taken of the family. Don't move."

Puzzled, Carol and Cam looked at each as they heard Issac in the next room opening and closing drawers. He emerged, holding an old black and white photo of a family.

"You have the same eyes as Polly, big like a doe." Issac handed the photo to Carol, smeared with blood from Issac's hand.

"Uncle Issac, she isn't related to us. She's the local librarian in Eden, a friend of mine. She's helping me with researching our family history."

"You sure, boy?" said he asked, his eyes narrowing into mere slits. "She looks so much like her. Pretty little thing," he said, cupping one hand to her chin and, in the process, smudging a bit of blood on her from his hand.

Quickly, Cam aligned his body between them. "I'm positive, Uncle Issac. Carol is a friend, not a relative. Jesus, you got blood on her." Reaching into his pocket, Cam tissued off the blood from her chin. "Carol, maybe you should wait in the car."

"Why you so interested in my family? Very few of us left. Am I right, Cam?" Issac said with a wink.

"I was asked to assist in…" Her voice hitched. "Researching the cape on Preston."

"Uncle Issac, I sold the old cape on Preston Road, the cape that was originally built by one of our ancestors, the Reverend Winters. The woman who bought the property is interested in the history of the place. Carol is merely helping her with the research."

"I see," Issac said. They looked on as he moved back to the kitchen table, picked up the knife, and continued skinning. Issac slowly licked some blood off his thumb, smiled, and looked directly at Carol with a piercing stare. "Who'd you say you were helping, girlie?"

"It's nobody local, Uncle Issac. The woman who bought the house moved up from Burlington."

"I see."

"Cam, I think I will wait outside. Give you some time alone with your uncle." Carol turned to Issac. "Thank you for your time."

"Anytime, sweetheart! Don't be a stranger now, doors always open," he mocked.

"Here are my keys. I'll meet you outside," Cam said.

Carol closed the door behind her.

"Pretty thing. Nosy, but pretty. She giving it up to you, boy?"

"She's not nosy, just a friend helping out. Here's my card. It has all my numbers on it. The person who bought the old cape is having dreams. Hell, I'm having dreams. Disturbing dreams, I think of our ancestor Reverend Winters. I read his mother Cyrene's diary. It's troubling. If you have any information that can shed some light on..." Cam stopped, noticing the carving knife pointed suddenly at his chest.

His uncle held the knife on him. From the tip, droplets of blood dripped, staining the old wooden floor as Issac roared. "Cyrene Winters was a fucking whore who killed her husband. A husband who provided. Ungrateful bitch. Same goes for the Reverend's wife, Polly. All of them, whores." Issac swiftly brought the knife down on the neck of the coyote. The crack from the knife's contact with bone rang out as blood poured, splattering Cam's leather oxfords.

"Jesus," Cam muttered as he stepped back and away from the table.

"Jesus won't help you here, boy. You're just like your father—a spineless, weak, pathetic excuse for a man. Get the hell out of my house and God help you if you ever come back."

Cam turned, opened the front door, and slammed it shut.

****

Cam found Carol in the front seat with the doors locked. He knocked on the passenger door, making her jump. Seeing him, she released the locks.

"Thank God, I wasn't sure you were coming out of there alive. Your uncle, he's, well, he's something else, my God, I've never..." she rambled.

"I know. I'm sorry, Carol. I had no idea. I should've known he'd be seriously fucked up. He is my father's brother, after all. Jesus, what an asshole."

"Yeah, but hey, it's okay, you couldn't have known."

"I should've known—he's related to me. My father wasn't any better. Again, I'm sorry."

"Forget it," she said, putting a hand to his. A movement in the woods caught her eye and had her shifting in her seat to get a better look.

"What is it, Carol?"

"I don't know. I thought I saw...I guess it's nothing."

"Are you sure?" he asked, turning back to her. He noticed the stray twig caught in her hair. "Wait, you have, a twig, just here," he said, reaching.

Her hand met his.

"Let me," he said, and gently released the twig from its web. With his hand, he smoothed the loose strands of her hair back in place behind her ear and met her eyes.

"We should probably get out of here before we end up on the menu," she joked.

"You're right, let's get the fuck out of here."

Chapter 44

The truth, Carol decided, was what they sought. She contemplated the steps she and Rebecca had taken in the research process as she walked around Rebecca's garden to the side door. Dropping the two grocery bags on the ground, she inched her fingers along the doorframe and found the key where Rebecca told her she would find it. Having unlocked the door, she picked up the groceries and stepped inside the large bright kitchen.

She decided to empty the contents on the large wooden table that sat in the middle of the room. Crossing the kitchen, she opened up the cupboard for a wine glass and poured a glass of the French Chablis that she purchased. She lifted the wine to her nose, breathed in the oaky scent with a hint of honey before sipping, and let out a satisfied sigh. She moved to the refrigerator, and paused, hearing the footsteps descending the stairs.

"Rebecca, I'm in the kitchen, I finished early at the library and decided to head over," Carol called. "I brought my laptop so we could review all of our notes with Cam when he gets here. I can't wait to tell you about the crazy visit to Cam's uncle's place. What a nut job! I seriously had my doubts that Cam and I were going to get out of there alive. His uncle is a real creep." Carol sipped her wine and considered. "In a way, though, I feel closer to Cam than I ever have. Do you want a glass of wine?" Carol paused at the sound of a door being opened. "Rebecca," she called as she moved toward the living room.

"Polly."

She jumped at the sound of his voice, startled to see the man standing in the shadow of the doorway, dressed in all black. She figured him to be in his late twenties. He wore a beard, light brown in color, and a braided ponytail fished down his back. She squinted and looked at him closer. something about him seemed familiar. "Do I know you?" Carol asked as the man placed a hand over the wood of the door, letting his fingers trail the shapes carved in the raised frame.

"I built this house."

"You built this house? I'm not sure I understand. This cape was built in 1820." Carol's breath hitched. Alarms echoed in her head as the man's eyes pierced hers, her fear rising from the crazed look in his eyes.

"I built this house for us, Polly, to raise our child in. That never happened, did it? You were *not* an obedient wife." His hand stroked the length of his beard as his eyes traveled down her body.

"I'm not sure who you are, but if you don't leave. I'm calling the police."

"I saw you, at the cabin, with my brother. I was standing at the edge of the woods, hidden. I knew who you were when I saw those big eyes of yours, and then I saw you sense me."

"Issac's cabin? I think you have me confused with someone else."

"I'm not confused. Stop pretending. You're my Polly. You came back to us."

"I'm not sure what you're talking about."

"You came back to me and Silence. We've waited patiently for you. You've returned to your husband where you belong. A fresh start, perhaps."

She saw it then, in the eyes, the blue eyes, the same eyes as Cam.

"I was at Cam's uncle's cabin. Camden Winters, are you related to Cam? And Issac?" She saw it then in his eyes, his confusion. The internal struggle as it played out in his mind trying to make sense of her words. He grabbed at his ears with his hands and shook his head back and forth. Almost in an attempt, she thought, to release her words from his head. He paced the length of the room, his eyes darting back at hers, the madness spilling over.

"Issac? Camden? You can't keep us straight, can you, Polly? You're still up to your old tricks. Once a whore…"

In a flash he was across the room, pinning her arm behind her back. His lips to her ear. "Where's the child?"

"Please, you're hurting me," Carol said using every ounce of her being to steady her voice.

"Don't play games with me. Where's the child? Your wicked child, that little whore Silence?"

"Silence?"

"I hear her. I hear her giggling, laughing. She's laughing at me again," he said, begging.

As he cupped his ears again, he released her arm. "You tell her to stop, Polly, or I swear that little bitch will be sorry when I find her. So will you."

Instinctively, Carol turned to run, but before she could, he slammed her body, with his full weight, against the side wall. She gasped at the stabbing pain exploding from her shoulder, her head woozy after the strike against the wall. In one swift movement, he threw her fully to the floor, the impact jarring her left kneecap, and she cried out.

"Tell me where the little bitch is hiding?" he yelled as he yanked her up by her hair. "Where's the little bitch hiding?" He screamed.

"I swear I don't know."

"You find her, Polly, and bring her to me. *Now!*" She stumbled as he threw her forward and released her.

Panicked, she quickly scanned the room, realizing her only choice was to start up the stairs.

"I will find her. I will make her stop. I promise."

As she reached the top of the landing, she listened for him. The silence fell over her like the dark. With sweat dripping from her brow, she tiptoed down the hall and paused at the sound of a woman whispering her name. With her ear to the bedroom door, she listened closer and reached for the doorknob. In the room, she found sheets of drywall lining the back wall. In the middle of the room sat a ladder and, next to the ladder, a utility knife. She quickly grabbed the knife, pocketed it, and turned toward the open door.

His hand suddenly around her mouth stifled the scream. His hands circled her neck, bearing down on her windpipe. She fought against his forearms as he dragged her body back into the hallway. She struggled to balance her weight against his. Desperate for air, she dug into his hands with her fingernails, ripped at his skin in an attempt to release his hands. Wheezing, her lungs on fire as the pressure swelled in her chest, she thrashed and kicked as she dug her fingernails even deeper into his skin. It was then she felt the warm stickiness of his blood on her fingers. The adrenaline in her body surged with the knowledge that she had hurt him.

Finally, he released his hands from her throat. She collapsed against him, her head rushing as the blackness filled her eyes. Her vision blurred in and out with each breath. The pain erupted in her chest as her throat swelled. Falling to her knees, she vomited the bloody bile from her throat.

Crouching alongside her body, his stale breath in her ear, his hand roamed up her back. "He likes it when you fight back," he said, petting her body like a dog. He moved to stand.

She kept her head down, gagged once more, the pain spreading throughout her body. She needed air to think and tried to push herself up. The kick from behind had her falling facedown against the floor.

He pulled her head back and ran a hand down her torso. His tongue rough and hot on her neck.

"He likes the salty taste of you, Polly," he said, his breath hot.

A wave of nausea washed over her again. Her panic grew as she sensed his growing arousal. He turned her body so that she faced him. She saw the evil, the challenge in his words. "Kiss me. Be a good girl, Polly, and kiss me." His lips were on hers, his tongue plunging into her mouth.

With all her strength, she pushed. As he fell back, his laughter roared in her ears. "You still have some fight in you. Good girl, the Reverend wants you to fight." He struck her hard, the impact of the blow throbbing behind her eyes.

The coppery metallic taste of blood filled her mouth as she blinked through the tears. A sneer of a smile covered his lips, his eyes filled with hunger. Carol knew at the moment that her survival depended on staying calm and playing along—pretending she was Polly.

He licked his lips and pulled her closer to him.

"Whores are not to be forgiven, Polly, but disciplined. You like being punished, don't you? God, in his infinite wisdom, spoke to me. Would you like to know what he said?"

On her knees, head bowed, she slowly slipped her hand into her pocket and felt the cold steel of the knife in her hand. She'd have one chance, and her life depended on it.

"Yes, I'd like to know," she whispered back, looking into his eyes.

"That I need to teach you how to be an obedient wife, Polly. You're like a child that needs to be punished in order to learn. I want to hear you say it. Tell me…"

The smirk on his face had her skin crawling, and with a faint voice, she answered him. "Yes, Reverend," she said as she moved her body closer to his. Carol saw then, in his face, the crazed excitement. With all the force she could muster, she plunged the knife deep into his stomach and watched his eyes as they bulged with shock.

He stared at her, bewildered. "Why, Polly?" He covered the steel end of the knife, protruding from his stomach, with his hand and with a scream pulled it from his body.

In shock, Carol stared as he stumbled and hit the

ground. Silence. He didn't move. She turned and ran down the stairs. When she reached the back door, she heard his screams. Stumbling off the back porch, she ran toward the woods and froze at the sound of the back door as it opened. Crouching low, she glanced back at the house and saw him. His face full of fury with eyes patrolling the back of the house, and one hand pressed against his stomach covered in a film of red blood. He lifted his head and sniffed the air while his eyes tracked the perimeter of the woods. "I'm going to rip you apart when I find you, Polly," he screamed. He stared straight in her direction, stumbled off the porch, and started into the woods after her.

Chapter 45

Finally home, Cam felt the weight of the day fall from his shoulders. He placed his keys in the bowl on the side table next to the door and noticed the flashing light on his office phone indicating he had messages. He intended to wait until he'd had a couple of sips of beer before he listened to work calls. He needed to take the edge off. A wave of anticipation danced through him when he thought about seeing Carol tonight at Rebecca's house.

He opened the refrigerator, twisted open a beer, and took a long swig. A satisfied sigh slipped from his lips. Thinking of the encounter with his uncle, Cam shuddered. *Crazy bastard,* he thought to himself as he loosened the tie around his neck. He crossed into his bedroom and took off his suit and tie and opted for his old LA Rams T-shirt and worn-in jeans for comfort, his home-wear. Opening the front door, he gathered his mail from the front stoop. He took another swig of his beer, leafed through his mail, and hit play on his answering machine.

"Message One—Cam, this is Lynn Curtis, I'm ready to make an offer on the condo on Elm Street, but I'd like to do another walk-through. I'm just not sure about the layout. Call me." Cam rolled his eyes in response and dropped his mail next to the machine. He took another drag off the beer.

"Message Two—Brother, I'm going home. I need to deal once and for all with the whore and her child. Pray to the Almighty, to the Lord Jesus Christ, for mercy on my soul." The voice sent a chill up Cam's spine. *What the hell?* If Cam believed in ghosts, he would've sworn it was his father's voice on his answering machine. Thank God his father was long dead, but then the question remained, whose voice was this?

Staring down at the machine, he replayed the message. He rubbed at the knots forming at the back of his neck as he listened, racked his brain trying to place the caller. *Who the hell is this?* "Fuck," he said, grabbing his keys and phone. Stopping, he turned back, retrieved the 9mm from the safe, and rushed out into the evening air.

In his car, Cam hit the contact on his phone for his mother. He needed answers and knew she'd be the only person who would have it besides Issac.

"Cam, are you alright?"

"I need your help. Do you know, did Uncle Issac have any children? Specifically, a male child?"

"Why do you ask?"

"Just answer the God damn question. I don't have time to fuck around, it's serious!"

"This isn't easy for me to talk about. I'm...not sure how to tell you this."

"What are you talking about?"

"Issac has one child, Jacob. You were three years old at the time when Jacob was born. I lied. I lied to your father."

"Lied about what, Mom?"

"I told your father, that..."

"Told him what?"

"I told him I had a stillbirth. That my baby was dead."

"What? Your baby?"

"Doc Adams helped me deliver the baby. He helped me keep the secret from your father. I gave the baby up. I gave the baby to Issac to raise."

"You? You what? Why would you ever give a baby to a sociopath like Issac?"

"I didn't have a choice. I haven't seen Jacob since Issac took him away. That was twenty-five years ago."

"I don't understand. Why would you give your child to Issac? Unless…you had an affair with Dad's brother."

"No! It wasn't like that!"

It was then that Cam heard her tears and the anguish in her voice. "If it wasn't an affair, Mom, then what was it?"

"Issac threatened your father that he would sell his share of the farm, unless…"

"Unless what, Mom?"

"They agreed on an arrangement. Your father bartered with Issac so that we could stay on the farm. To have a roof over our head."

"You're saying that he made an arrangement to barter his own wife?"

"Cam, I had no choice. If I'd fought back, Issac and your father would have…"

"Hurt you," he finished her sentence.

Just then the memory creeped in, like a punch to the gut. Cam standing in the doorway as his father held a gun to his mother's head. Threatening to shoot her, while his uncle raped her. "Jesus, Mom," he whispered.

"I learned to get it over with, learned it was useless to fight back. When I became pregnant, your father became even more abusive to me and…to you. I think your father knew the baby was Issac's. Issac left me alone after I gave him the child."

"Why didn't you ever tell me?"

"Oh, Camden, how was I supposed to tell my only son that his father prostituted his mother out for rent? There's so much I'm ashamed of. Ashamed I wasn't strong enough to protect you and just leave."

Hearing her words, Cam thought to himself, *But I'm not your only son. I'm just the only son you claim.* "I need to go and clean up this mess."

"Cam, what are you talking about? What mess?"

"I just hope it's not too late," he said and hung up.

Chapter 46

Jack hoisted the hundred-pound bag of dog food into the bed of his truck. The sight of the three dogs sitting in the back row of the pickup, heads out the window, made him smile. His grin widened as he spotted Rebecca coming out of the feed store. His heart skipped a beat as she crossed the parking lot toward him. When she reached the truck, he noticed the worry on her face.

"Jack, we gotta go, something's wrong at the house. Carol's in trouble!"

He quickly closed the gate on the pickup. "Did you try calling her cell?"

"I left my phone in the truck charging," she said, as she climbed into the passenger seat, unplugged her phone, and hit Carol's contact. "Jack, we have to hurry. She's afraid. I can feel her fear. Someone is hurting her."

"Any luck with the call?"

"It keeps going to voicemail. I'm scared, Jack."

Rebecca leaned her head back against the car seat and closed her eyes.

"I see a man with his hands around her throat. She can't breathe."

In the backseat, Max began to whine. "Maxie, it's okay, boy," she soothed.

"I'll place a call to the State Police to do a well-check visit?"

"Good idea, yes, please hurry. Please God, let Carol be okay," she prayed.

"Anything?" he asked.

"No, still voicemail. Any luck with the State Police?"

"They're on the way. I told them we are in route. We'll get to her."

"We have to get to her before it's too late. I can see what he's doing."

Jack reached for her hand.

"Jack, he's hurting her. She's having trouble breathing," she said, closing her eyes for a brief moment.

"We'll get there."

"Jack, I know what she's experiencing, the evil. The being scared out of your mind madness, knowing you're going to die. I feel for her. The memories of my abduction and of Allison are coming too fast. I can't control them."

"Rebecca, listen to me. You're the strongest woman I know. We're going to get to her. We're not going to let Carol die."

"Okay, okay."

"In the glove compartment is a pencil and my notebook. Can you get it out?" he asked.

"Yes, but why?"

"I want you to write down everything you're seeing and feeling. It might help us help Carol." *And also might distract you,* he thought to himself.

She did exactly what he suggested and wrote exactly what she saw. "The man has a long beard. He's tall, a bit shorter than you. He's young, maybe early to mid-twenties. He's dressed in all black. Carol's running through the woods, she's trying to hide. The man he's, he's..." She stopped.

"He's what?!"

"He's hunting her," she whispered back.

"Hunting her? Jesus," he said.

"I hear Carol calling him..."

"Calling him what, Rebecca?"

"Reverend."

Chapter 47

Carol struggled to get her footing on the damp leaves as she made her way along the edge of the woods. She heard him in the distance. Heard the roar of him in her head. The screaming, the harshness of his voice yelling for Polly—screaming for the whore. She searched for anything familiar, a stone wall, a path, anything that might lead her to safety. She veered off to the left and retreated deeper yet into the woods.

She sought temporary cover behind the big gray boulder that sat alone in the field of trees. She saw him behind every tree. Her mind played tricks on her. Trembling from the cold, she rubbed her hands together before scouring the ground in front of her. She searched the ground for an object, a weapon, anything she could use to defend herself.

Panic spread deep in her chest. She paused and put a hand to her heart, an attempt to calm the pounding. Breathing deeply, she steadied herself and prepared for the fight to survive. She rested her back against the cold surface of the rock, kept her body erect, and listened for him. She heard nothing but the wind rustling the leaves in the trees above her and the sound of water rippling in the brook. It was then she heard it, the approaching footsteps, and knew it was time.

Terrified, she plastered her body against the boulder and listened. Holding her back straight like a statue, she focused her breathing. *Keep it together. Keep it together. You have to outsmart this asshole.* For a brief second, she let her eyes close, and suddenly a hand on her shoulder had her dropping to her knees and scrambling. Frantic, she scurried on all fours across the wet forest floor, away, away, away. She turned and raised the branch over her head in defense. It was then she saw the eyes. The piercing blues staring back at her. She raised the branch higher, squinted, and saw Cam. With his finger to his lips, he motioned for her to stay down.

Cam knelt next to her and pulled the 9mm from the back of his pants. He checked the chamber, stopped, and cocked an ear to listen. They looked at each other as they heard the sound of footsteps on leaves. He was getting closer. Cam grabbed her hand. "We need to keep moving. Can you walk?" he breathed.

With a silent nod, she took his arm, and he pulled her to stand. Together, they moved deeper into the woods to the brook. His arm held her as he guided her across the shallow waters of the brook. The cold water snapped the fear clear out of her. Reaching the other side, they stopped and sat against a large oak to catch their breath. Cam saw the bruises forming on her face. The angry colors of purple and red pooling underneath her skin. He placed his gun in front of him. "Let me," he said and gently wiped the dried leaves caked in blood from her cheek. He didn't hear the man behind him. Her scream echoed through the woods at the sight of the man in black lunging for Cam. In a split second, she grabbed the gun and pulled the trigger.

A direct hit. Carol let the gun fall to the ground. The bullet's impact threw the man back slightly, a tree stopping his fall. He stumbled forward, regained his footing, and lunged again.

"Jacob! Stop!" Cam yelled.

Jacob looked at Cam with eyes full of confusion.

"Brother, is that you?" he asked, before lunging again.

****

In the direction of the scream, Jack and Rebecca made their way through the woods. At the sound of another gunshot, Jack pulled Rebecca to him.

"Jesus, Jack, where is she?" Rushing through the woods, they found them by the large oak. Rebecca ran to a shaken Carol, who sat in a heap under the tree, staring out, in shock.

"I shot him. I shot him," she cried when she saw Rebecca's face.

Rebecca kneeled on the ground and wrapped an arm around her. "You're safe now. It's over."

A man lay writhing on the ground. Fresh blood pooled in the dry leaves around the man's body. Cam stood and held the gun to the man's temple.

"Cam, the State police are on their way," Jack said calmly.

"I should end you now, Jacob, you crazy piece of shit," Cam shouted, his grip tightening around the gun.

"Jacob?" Rebecca said, "Cam, who is he? Who's Jacob?"

"This piece of shit is my half-brother," he sneered.

"Cam, he's not worth it," Jack said, inching closer to Cam's body. "Come on, man, you know he's not worth it."

"Jack, I'm sick of this shit. It needs to end. I need to end it now," Cam said as he cocked the gun.

"Come on, Brother, you're a killer like all the rest of us. Pull the trigger, I dare you." Jacob taunted, his teeth clenched in pain.

Jack placed his hand on the top of the gun. "Cam, you don't want to do this. Don't listen to him."

"I'm ending this, Jack."

"Cam, he's lost his mind. He's not worth it. You're not a killer. You're nothing like this piece of shit," Jack said, slowly bringing the gun down.

Chapter 48

"How's Carol?" Jack asked as Rebecca entered the kitchen.

"Doc Adams is examining her. She's badly bruised. He plans to give her a sedative so she can sleep. After the sedative takes effect, she should be out until morning. I told Carol that we would all be here, spending the night, so that nobody's alone. She's shaken up, but the swelling around her throat is going down with the compress. Where's Cam?" Rebecca moved to the stove to pull out the lasagna.

"He's in the living room talking on his cell to the State Police. They called earlier to update him on the standoff at the cabin with his uncle."

"Standoff?"

"It seems his Uncle Issac didn't take too kindly to the law showing up at his place."

"Can this day be over yet?" Rebecca said, pulling the salad out of the refrigerator.

"Issac pulled a rifle on the State Police when they showed up at his cabin. From the sounds of it, he barricaded himself in the cabin with the semi-automatic rifle."

As Cam walked into the kitchen, Rebecca felt the heaviness of his exhaustion in her body as she set a wine glass in front of him.

"Thanks," he said with a half-smile as she poured a

generous glass of wine. "In true Winters fashion, Issac pulled the rifle on them, so they shot him. Issac's dead."

"Jesus, Cam," Jack said.

"Cam, I'm sorry," she said.

"I can't say I'm sorry, Rebecca. My uncle was a very sick man who raised a very sick son. To know that his son was my half-brother makes my stomach turn. At least now they can't hurt anybody."

"Cam, I never knew you had a half-brother."

"Me either, until earlier today when I called my mother. I asked her if Uncle Issac had any children. She told me the whole fucked-up story. Seems, my father prostituted my mother out to his brother in exchange for rent. A not so pretty backwoods hillbilly soap opera."

"Oh, Cam, your poor mother."

"Oh yeah, Rebecca, '*my poor mother*.' She chose to stay with him. She could've saved herself and me a lot of pain if she'd only left his sorry ass years ago." Cam grunted.

"Camden, you have no idea what your mother went through. Show some respect, son," Doc Adams said as he entered. "Your mother was so beaten down, so very lost—a shell of a human being. I delivered Jacob. In all my years that delivery is one that I will never, ever forget. It haunts me to this day. Your mother came to my office in the middle of the night and begged me to keep it a secret. She begged me to say the baby was stillborn. She knew if she brought the baby home, your father would hurt the baby like he hurt you. She cried throughout the whole delivery. Wailed, not just for the baby, but for you and the abuse you received. She refused to hold, hell, even to look at the baby after the birth. I promised her I would keep her secret. I hope, one day, you can come to understand the choice I made and why. Believe it or not, Camden, she loves you."

"Understand the choice?" Cam said with hard eyes.

"Yes, Camden, I kept your mother's secret. I helped her. She lived in horrible circumstances and had minimal options. Her only concern was you."

"I lived in those circumstances too, Doc, every fucking day. Excuse me if I'm a bit pissy about it all."

"I know you did, son."

"And you! How could you hand the baby over to Issac? Knowing who Issac was," Cam said, eyes hard.

"Camden, I tried to talk your mother into putting the baby up for adoption, but she wouldn't hear of it. She'd made an agreement with Issac, she'd give him the baby in exchange for the house. Issac was the baby's father. I had no choice. I saw the look of fear in your mother's eyes when Issac came into the room. She was terrified of him. I knew, at that moment, that Issac had hurt her. I am not a violent man, but I threatened him as he took that baby in his arms. Heard him pronounce that his son shall be called Jacob. He didn't say a word to me. He wrapped the baby up and left."

"Well, Doc, here's a bit of news for you. I just got off the phone with the State's criminal psychologist. She believes that Issac and Jacob had some sort of shared delusional disorder—they were fixated on this house and its owners."

"I am sorry for Jacob, not only how he came into the world but what he endured. Camden, I will never forgive myself for being part of sacrificing a baby, but I didn't see another choice."

"Well, I suppose we all have some burden to bear.

Jacob didn't need to turn out the way he did. Look at me, Doc. We all know my father was no saint. I didn't repeat his history, nor do I plan to start. I need to work on letting go of the past. Starting with finding a way to forgive my mother." Cam made a slight snorting sound as he put his head down. Doc reached out, laid a hand on the back of his head. Cam met Doc's eyes and nodded.

"Cam, what did the psychologist mean by a shared fixation?" Jack asked.

"The police located an entire outbuilding on Issac's property filled with pictures of the house taken over the past forty-odd years. They also found a detailed journal outlining their beliefs. Issac started watching the cape decades ago and brought his son into it. Both Issac and Jacob believed that Polly and Silence had come back from the dead to haunt them. Given the number of photos, the police believe Issac and Jacob recently turned their attention on you, Rebecca. You being young and female increased Issac and Jacob's obsessive behavior and delusional thinking. From the pictures on the walls, both were taking turns watching you. After Issac met Carol, they fixated on her, believing she was Polly reincarnated because of her physical resemblance to Polly."

"Oh my God!" Rebecca cried.

Jack circled his arms about her. "You were right, all those times you felt like you were being watched," Jack said, holding her tighter.

"The cops also found pictures of Carol coming in and out of the library and pictures of Carol at home. They believe Issac convinced Jacob that Carol was Polly, which was why they focused on her."

"Cam, I'm sorry you have to deal with all this."

"I'm the one who is sorry. Sorry to have sold you this cursed house. Sorry that Carol was hurt. Sorry that I didn't know my relatives were crazy, violent, and dangerous predators. I swear I didn't know what they were up to."

Jack reached over and squeezed Cam's shoulder. "You gotta let it go, man, none of us believe you were part of this. Carol is going to be okay."

"Cam, as hard as this is to say, Issac and Jacob were right about one thing."

"What do you mean? Right about what?" Cam said, confused.

"Polly and Silence, since I moved in here, the dreams, the giggling, the little blonde girl dripping wet from a swim. All of these things were signs, warning me to pay attention. The dreams were showing me, showing us, that danger lurked in the woods, at the pond, and in the shadows. Through the dreams, Polly and Silence not only revealed their story but, I believe, were warning us that the threat still existed."

"So you think Polly and Silence were haunting Issac and Jacob?"

"I don't know if haunting is the right word. I'd like to think that Polly and Silence were seeking justice. They kept watch over this house, peacefully, but in watching they knew that evil lurked. If Jacob and Issac's intention was to continue the Reverend's legacy of violence, well, I think Polly and Silence tried very hard to protect us all. And in the end, they did just that. And Cam, for the record, I love this house. I'm thankful for their watchful eyes over me. But I'm also very thankful this is over."

****

That night, Rebecca fell asleep with Jack's arms tightly around her. She dreamed of the pond, of Polly holding her daughter Silence. A mother cradling her daughter, rocking her back and forth. Both, finally, at peace, no longer struggling to be heard.

Chapter 49

Carol woke to find Cam in the chair by her bed, asleep, his hand holding hers. Her body ached, the stiffness had settled in, and she felt bruised from head to toe. She gingerly let her hand travel across her face and winced. Felt her right eyebrow covered in raised stitches. As she shifted her body in the bed, she groaned, and Cam's eyes flew open.

"Are you okay? What do you need? Another painkiller?" he said, jumping up.

"No, no, I'm okay." Her voice was shaky. She winced as she sat up and fought against the tears. *I'm stronger than this.*

"Are you sure?" he queried, adjusting the pillows behind her.

"Yes, just stiff and bruised. You look like you didn't get much rest. Did you sleep in that chair all night?"

"Yeah, but I'm fine. The chair is more comfortable than it looks." He sat down on the edge of the bed and took ahold of her hand.

She noticed his worried expression as he studied her bruises. "Cam, I'm going to be fine. I'm not easily broken."

"Carol, there's a lot I need to tell you."

"So tell me."

"First, I need to thank you for saving my life. If it

wasn't for you, I don't think either one of us would be here. How can I…?" He paused hearing the door open.

Rebecca entered, tray in hand, with Lulu on her heels. "I thought I heard you two up. I hope you're hungry. I brought breakfast."

"Thanks, Rebecca, that smells good. I don't know about Carol, but I could eat."

"Please, God, coffee first," Carol entreated.

With Lulu nestled at the foot of the bed, Rebecca poured a cup from the pot and handed it to Carol. The sweet woody fragrance of cinnamon filled her nostrils as she sipped. "Oh my God, this coffee is better than painkillers."

"Speaking of painkillers, Doc Adams is here. He'd like to come up after you've finished breakfast to examine you." Rebecca rested the tray of food on the bed.

"That's fine. I'm really okay, my body aches, nothing that time won't heal," she said as she rolled her bruised shoulder. "I think I'll avoid mirrors for a while. I expect I have some nasty bruises."

"You're beautiful, bruises and all," Cam said.

"Cam's right, you're beautiful, and I'm glad you're okay," Rebecca said as she leaned over to kiss her forehead.

"Like I told Cam, I'm going to be fine."

"I know you will be. Cam, can you give Carol and me a minute?"

"Sure, I'll be right back." He gave Carol's hand a squeeze before leaving the room.

"Carol, I wanted to apologize for not being here yesterday when you arrived. Jack and I were running late and stopped for dog food."

"Rebecca, I was the one who was early to your house. It's nobody's fault. I survived. Jacob was coming for me. He believed I was Polly. Jacob wouldn't have stopped until he found me."

"I know that's true, but still I can't stop thinking about…"

"I was damn lucky, not just for Cam finding me in those woods, but for finding out how damn strong I really am. I've been living my life on hold for a long time. Not anymore. I'm done not living, not taking chances. If I've learned anything from this experience, it's to live while you can because you never know when you can lose it all."

With a soft knock, Cam poked his head back in. "All set?" he asked.

"All set, Cam," Rebecca answered.

"I will say, I'm glad it's over. I think it's going to be a while before I can go into the woods again."

"Carol, if you're up to it, the State Police would like to come by to get your statement. If you're too tired, I can hold them off," Cam informed her.

"No, I'd like to get it over with. The sooner I can put this behind me, the better."

"When the State Police get here, I'd like to sit in. If that's okay with you, Carol?" he asked.

"I'd appreciate it, Cam, thank you. I need all the support I can get. I don't think my mind has caught up with everything that's happened. I know I shot Jacob, but it all feels like a blur. I feel a bit numb." She raised her cup to her lips and sipped. "By the way, what happened to Jacob?" A strained look passed between Cam and Rebecca.

"He was taken by the State Police to the Burlington

Medical Center for treatment for his wounds. When he's stable enough, the police will transfer him to a locked psychiatric facility for assessment down in southern Vermont," he offered.

"Carol, Jacob can't hurt us anymore."

"I should've made sure of that. I still regret not blowing the bastard away. That piece-of-shit needs to be locked up for life and the key thrown away."

"Like Rebecca said, Cam, Jacob can't hurt us," Carol soothed, reaching for his hand.

"I'm going to leave you two and head down to the kitchen. I'll send Doc Adams up when he's done with his breakfast."

"Thanks, Rebecca, not only for the food but everything."

"You get some rest, Carol, we have a lot to be thankful for. Cam, can I talk to you in the hall for a moment?"

"Sure." He squeezed Carol's hand. "I'll be right back."

Rebecca and Cam eased out into the hall. Rebecca softly closed the bedroom door behind them.

"Cam, I just wanted to take a minute and say that you're doing a great job taking care of her. Thank you for that."

"Thanks, Rebecca. I'm not sure I deserve thanks though. A big part of me feels responsible for getting her into this mess. My fucked-up family is why she's lying in that bed. She saved my life out there."

"Nobody could have predicted this...you're good for her."

"She's special. I'm glad to do it."

"She is special. I also wanted to say...tread

carefully."

"What do you mean?"

"If you haven't noticed, Carol's got a heart that's been bruised some. I care about both of you, so, again, tread carefully. Okay?"

"A bruised heart, well, I figure that's something Carol and I have in common. Message received."

"Thanks, now I better get downstairs and see what the rest of the troops need."

****

As Cam opened the bedroom door, he found her fast asleep. He eased his body down quietly on the other side of the bed, took her hand in his, and soon found himself drifting off. The dream came quickly, him and Carol holding hands, walking down the path toward the pond. Upon reaching the pond, they found them. A young mother and daughter sat on the bank looking out. The daughter's body rested back against her mother's. The mother turned and smiled up at Cam. He smiled back and shook his head in understanding. A look of peace filled the mother's face as she held her child.

Chapter 50

November 2016

Rebecca stood at the kitchen window, sipping a cup of jasmine tea, taking a few minutes for herself, a much-needed break from her family who'd come for a visit. She loved them all, but having a full house was exhausting. Lulu rubbed her head against Rebecca's leg as Rebecca sipped and gazed out at her family. It tickled her to see her father and her brothers standing in the backyard with Jack. All the men stood circled around her newly purchased used John Deere tractor. She shook her head and laughed as she watched her brother Rory kick one of the tractor's tires, which had the other males nodding with approval. *Why? Why do men feel the need to kick tires? What could it possibly tell them about the value of my tractor?* Her dad and brothers were most likely debating the pros and cons of her purchase.

Rebecca's dogs lay on the grass, and Jack's dog, Keeper, followed suit, holding watch over the men. Her mom joined her at the sink and looked out to see her husband and sons with Jack and pulled her daughter in close.

"Mom, can I get you some tea?"

"No, sweetie, I'm good. Your brothers are probably giving your Jack a hard time out there."

"Most likely, but Jack can handle it."

"I like him."

"That's good. I can honestly say he's the first man I've dated who truly understands my heart."

"Well, that definitely makes him a keeper. Have you told him about...?"

"Yes, he knows all about my history and gift. He's trying very hard to understand it all."

"Well, then he most certainly is a keeper."

"He is. You wouldn't believe one of his sisters though—Maureen, she's a real piece of work."

"There's one in every family. A real pill, huh?"

"Yes, she's a pill alright, with red hair to boot."

"I'm sure my girl can handle her." Her mom pointed out the window. "You said he was cute, but he's really adorable."

Rebecca nodded in agreement, watching as her father put an arm around Jack, and felt a warmth overflow her heart.

"Looks like your father is warming up to him. I like him a lot, your Jack."

"Thanks, Mom. I'm in love with him."

"Oh, honey, that's what I've been praying for. Does it scare you?"

"Yes, but in a good way."

"Well, when it scares you, you know he's the one. Extra bonus, he gives great hugs."

"That's not all he's great at," she said, laughing as her mother wiggled her eyebrows at her.

"Good, I'm glad he's taking care of my daughter's needs. Everybody needs a cup of good love."

They both turned, hearing an eruption of hysterical crying and screaming echoing down the hall from the living room.

"Grandma, Grandma! Aiden won't give me my cards back," Rebecca's niece, Olivia, screamed.

"I'm on it," her mom said as she headed to the living room to break up the fight. Turning back, she said over her shoulder, "You'd better get out there and save your man from being tortured. God only knows what they're putting him through."

Rebecca grabbed her sweater and headed out the side door. She found her brothers grilling Jack and stifled a laugh as she listened.

"Rory, he drives a Ford," Sean said, as he checked out Jack's pickup. Rory turned and gave Jack a thumbs-up.

"Okay, Sean, he made it through door one."

"Door? What do you mean?" Jack said, puzzled.

"Not door, Jack, but doors," Rory said as he approached Jack, throwing an arm around his shoulder and pulling him in tightly. "Only ninety-nine doors to go."

Jack's pleading eyes found Rebecca. Rory and Sean erupted into laughter seeing his look of terror. Rebecca tried to stifle her giggle but gave up and joined her brothers. "Jack, they're only kidding. Knock it off, you two idiots. Dad, tell Rory and Sean to knock it off."

"Okay guys, you heard your sister, knock it off."

"Don't worry, Jack, like Rebecca said, we're kidding. Really, there's only one rule that matters to us."

"What's that?" Jack asked.

"*You* hurt her, *we* kill you. Understood?" Rory glared and pulled Jack in tighter.

"Understood. I wouldn't have it any other way."

Jack extended his hand, and both men shook on it.

"Good. I'm glad we reached an understanding."

"Okay, guys, leave him alone."

"Not a chance, little sister. Jack can handle it," Sean retorted.

"Besides, Rebecca, he's going to need to have steel balls to deal with the chain you're going to have around his neck."

"I'll wear it proudly," Jack said with a wink.

"Auntie Becca!"

Rebecca turned to see her brother Rory's oldest daughter, Olivia, bolt across the yard toward her. Olivia's moon-shaped face was bright with excitement. Rebecca opened her arms for a bear hug.

"Hey, sweet-pea, you having fun?"

"I love it here! Silence told me all about swimming in the pond and how you were saved. Can I come back next summer and swim? Please!"

"What? You talked with Silence?"

"Sure, I know all about ghosts. Kimmie in my class had a ghost living in her house, and she bragged all about it. Kimmie's going to be *so* jealous when I tell her about talking with Silence. Kimmie's ghost was pretty boring. She never talked, just walked around. Silence likes to talk a lot!"

"What else did Silence talk about?"

"Let me think. Oh, she said her mama's happy now. There's no reason to be scared, the bad men are gone. She's happy you live in her house. She likes you. I told her my Auntie Becca is the best. She wants you to plant a butterfly garden and…"

"Wow, it sounds like you had quite the conversation. I'm still getting used to Silence and her mama living with me."

"It's no big deal, Aunt Becca. Silence loves Manny and Maxie. She said Lulu is still a scaredy cat, but she hopes to make friends with her soon. She also likes Jack and Keeper."

"Well, I'm glad," Rebecca said with a slight laugh, realizing that for Olivia, having a ghost in her aunt's house was, like Olivia said, "no big deal." It tickled her how accepting her niece was of Silence. *Adults could learn a thing or two from children.*

"Olivia!" Aiden screamed, kicking a soccer ball toward them.

"I gotta go play with Aiden. I promised Grandma I would since I hit him for taking my cards," she said, boasting a naughty grin.

"Well, you better go do what Grandma said before she catches you talking to me. Hey, and Olivia, be nice!" Rebecca smiled after her, as her niece kicked the soccer ball hard across the grass to Aiden as they set off to play.

****

Having said goodbye to her family, Jack and Rebecca made their way to town for a quick bite at the local diner. As the sun began to set, beautiful streaks of pinks and oranges painted the sky. The peaceful scene settled in her soul. She reached for Jack's hand, and, with gazes meeting, her heart skipped.

"I want to spend the rest of my days with you, Rebecca McCabe," he said, his brown eyes misting with emotion as he brought her hand to his lips.

The tender words had her eyes filling with emotion too. "Jack, me too, the rest my days." Holding his hand in hers, Rebecca closed her eyes as the image formed.

An image of Jack hoisting a little girl with long brown hair onto his shoulders. The little girl giggling, all three of them at the pond, soaked from a swim. The little girl in a bikini pointed a finger at her Mama's tummy.

"Daddy, I'm going to be a big sister."

A very pregnant Rebecca beamed as she rubbed her hand across her big belly. Waiting for the sensation of a baby's kick.

"Yes, you are! My big girl!" Jack exclaimed.

"No, Daddy! Not big girl. Big sister!" she said defiantly.

"Sorry, yes, big sister! You are going to be an awesome big sister. Now it's time for us to get back to the house and put you and Mommy down for your naps."

"When I'm a big sister I won't have to take naps anymore. Right, Daddy?"

"Let's cross that bridge when we come to it," he said, smiling at his daughter.

"What bridge, Daddy?"

"Yeah, Daddy, what bridge?" Rebecca restated winking at her husband.

"Well, the nap bridge of course, you silly girls," Jack said as he hoisted his daughter onto his shoulders and reached out with the other hand to hold his waddling wife.

"Daddy, I've never heard of a nap bridge. Are you making it up?"

"I'll tell you all about it when I tuck you in," he said as the family made their way down the path under a canopy of green leaves to home.

A word about the author...

Maria D'Haene is a social worker, children's author, and screenwriter. She published her first children's book, "Who is Making a Mess?" in 2020. Currently, she has two scripts optioned, "Hidden Christmas" and "Love, Apples." She is a Stowe Story Lab grant recipient for her script "Broken."